Doing horoscopes was an interesting hobby, but she hadn't realized it could put her life in danger...

Christy shot a glance at the hall mirror and smoothed her hair. At the door she called out, "Who is it?"

"Emilina Perez. You did my horoscope two weeks ago. I have some questions."

Christy opened the door as wide as the chain lock would allow and peered out. "It's a little late, Ms. Perez. You should have called first. Usually, I meet clients at a public place, like a restaurant or the park—" Christy glanced at the woman's attire. "—or maybe a bar. I don't do business at my home."

"I lost your phone number, but I had your address." The woman leveled her dark, penetrating eyes. "I drove all the way from Faller to talk to you. I don't understand some of this shit in my chart. I paid you, so you gotta explain it to me."

Christy stared through the gap in the doorway with only a chain separating her from the woman's intimidations. But as she watched, the lids came half-way down on Emilina's eyes and a lazy smile softened her features. The woman shrugged. "Look, if you can't talk right now, okay, I understand. But it was a long drive over here, and I really gotta pee—at least let me use the toilet before I leave."

Christy felt guilty for being so cautious. Suspicion

was a side effect of working at the sheriff's department, but she understood a full bladder. Muttering "Just a second," she closed the door and unchained it.

The door burst open. Heavy hands grabbed her by the T-shirt. Two men wearing sunglasses and baseball caps pulled low over their foreheads slammed her up against the wall. Emilina stood to one side.

"Do everything I say or you'll get hurt. Do you understand?" said the one with the black, bushy beard.

On a blazing July day in California's San Joaquin Valley, snitch Johnny Blue is murdered by a lethal heroin injection. Undercover narcotic detective James Wolfe, the operative who handled Blue, goes to the sheriff's department substation seeking ex-girlfriend Christy Bristol. In the past, he ridiculed her hobby of casting horoscopes. Now he needs her expertise to catch the man he suspects is behind Blue's murder, a drug dealer named Lloyd Parr. Stuck on the lowest rung of law enforcement, Christy becomes first a victim, then a hero, in the high-stakes game of narcotic trafficking. Through her eyes, the drug world is reduced to individual players, lost values, and discarded dreams. The reality of what goes on in the fertile land of the San Joaquin Valley is far more disturbing than the Hollywood version of drug lords and a wealthy lifestyle fueled by drug money. In the drug world of the Valley, there are no winners. Only losers.

KUDOS for *Fools Rush In*

"The first in the series, the story is well written, tense, and exciting. You'll be riveted from the very first page." ~ Taylor Jones, Reviewer

"On reading this book, one realizes that the author, in her former life working for the sheriff's department, must have come into contact with a lot of really creepy characters. And, when Christy is kidnapped by some of these dangerous people, my heart pounded right along with hers. There's a poignant scene, one of my favorites, when she's sure that she's going to be murdered, and she longingly looks out over the Valley landscape and prepares herself for a quick death with a thought that she should 'remember this.' Not to spoil the ending, but her musings are later what gets the case solved, and Christy lives to enjoy another day." ~ All Mystery eNewsletter

"Frazier does an excellent job keeping the reader on the edge of the seat." ~ Lesa Holstine, The Bookbitch

"Frazier skillfully combines drugs, murder, law enforcement, and astrology to create a chilling tale of drug lords and their victims, set in the beautiful San Joaquin Valley, home of vineyards, wineries, and meth labs. The story will grab your attention and hold it from beginning to end." ~ Regan Murphy, Reviewer

"Christy is a great character. Told almost entirely from her viewpoint, we can't help but feel her fear and cheer her on. She is strong and clever and thinks fast on her feet. This series can go in a lot of directions and I plan to be there to see what comes next." ~ Kim Reis, Armchair Reviews

ACKNOWLEDGEMENTS

Special thanks to JT Ford, the men of Eastside NET, EJ Allison, Della Sandoval, Cathy Perez, and all the women who work without praise or recognition at their desks in law enforcement and other "pink collar" jobs.

FOOLS RUSH IN

Christy Bristol Mysteries
Book 1

Sunny Frazier

A Black Opal Books Publication

FOOLS RUSH IN
Copyright © 2010 by Sunny Frazier
Cover Design by Jackson Cover Design
All cover art copyright © 2016
All Rights Reserved
Print ISBN: 978-1-626945-58-6

First Publication: MAY 2010

Published by Black Opal Books **http://www.blackopalbooks.com**

DEDICATION

To my father, RO Frazier, for the talent;
To my mother, Peggy O'Hara Frazier, for the sass;
To my sister, Catherine, for her support;
And to Lottie, who watches over us.

"For fools rush in where angels fear to tread."
~ Alexander Pope, *An Essay on Criticism*

Mars is the catalyst.

CHAPTER 1

John Ballew lifted his eyelids and looked around the room. Faded green curtains danced in slow motion away from the window. A spider on the sill hung precariously on the strands of a web. Time slowed to a dusty crawl. The young man licked his lips with great effort and relished the sensation of his tongue against the dryness.

"How you doing, Johnny Blue?"

Ballew tracked his eyes to a figure in one corner of the room. A face grinned down at him, showing large, yellowed teeth. Another face, this one hidden in a mass of black hair, appeared next to it.

"How much did you give him?"

"Enough to make him think he's on his way to heaven."

Ballew could make out the voices, but the words

themselves made no sense. It really didn't matter. Sound drifted through the thick air and bobbed up and down in the currents, like the green curtain. He let his eyes go back to the window.

"Do ya wanna go to heaven, Johnny Blue?"

The Faces wanted something from him, but Ballew couldn't understand what that something was. He wanted the Faces to either join him in this soft-focus world or leave. Again, he licked his lips, but his tongue had gone dry. His eyes were dry too, and he was aware of the weight of his eyelids. If he closed his eyes completely, the Faces would go away.

"Seein' any angels yet?"

His eyelids were so heavy, they pulled his head down. He felt his neck lose muscle and bone as his head swelled and increased in weight. His chin descended toward his breastbone, but the neck stretched and held.

One arm hung loosely across his body. He didn't know where his other arm was, and he was too tired to look for it. He followed the muted colors of a snake tattoo that slithered up his inner forearm. Between the fork of the snake's tongue was the needle. The plunger was down and the syringe was empty.

It was the last thing John Ballew saw.

ℰ✧ℰ✧

The primer gray Ford LTD turned down a dusty road

and pulled up sharply in front of a mobile home half-hidden in a nectarine orchard. Without waiting for the dust to settle, two men got out. The driver reached back into the car and furiously pressed on the horn.

"Damn informants," fumed the bearded man as he gave up on the horn and stood waiting in the driveway. "I told him eleven o'clock at the Texaco station on McCall and 186."

His partner scratched the stubble of a new beard. "Probably out partying last night."

The driver walked to the front door of the trailer and took the steps two at a time. "Johnny Blue, get your ass out of bed. We've got work to do."

He started to knock on the door, but it swung open at his touch. He was immediately aware of a stench emanating from the doorway and the sound of buzzing flies.

"Whew, what died?" asked his partner, coming up behind him.

"Let's hope it's not Blue."

They drew their .45s and slowly entered the trailer.

With the air conditioner off and the summer sun beating down on the metal roof, the mobile home was easily ninety degrees inside. The air was dense with the smell of decay. Flies concentrated on an object hanging on the opposite wall.

"What the hell—

Impaled on the wall above a cluttered dining room

table was the carcass of a large rat. Written above the vermin, presumably in its own blood, was the word "Blue."

"Wolfman," the partner said, as he put a hand on the other narc's shoulder, "you are in some deep shit this time."

CHAPTER 2

The temperature topped 105 degrees for the twelfth day in a row. The San Joaquin Valley was a pressure cooker, surrounded by mountains that pushed the heat back onto the California flatlands until tempers exploded. Office Assistant III Christy Bristol sat at her desk in the sheriff's department substation and stared at the heat waves rippling off the asphalt. Whenever the thermometer skyrocketed past 100 it seemed to ignite the worst in people. The stack of paperwork piled on her desk was proof. There were more Assault with a Deadly Weapon reports in the past two weeks than she'd seen all year, as people went after each other with knives, guns, and whatever else they got their hands on. Crimes of summer were crimes of passion and hate, all too often escalating to PC 187—Murder.

Christy slipped off her glasses and pushed aside the

lank, brown bangs covering her forehead. Only ten in the morning and she was already wringing wet. The air conditioner, set at seventy-two degrees, fought a losing battle with the gusts of furnace-hot air that rushed in every time the door opened. Deputies streamed into the station, seeking Gatorade and trying to avoid heat stroke in their bulletproof vests. The thirty-man facility baked in unshaded isolation among countless rows of Thompson Seedless grapevines, sixteen miles southwest of headquarters in downtown Kearny. Christy, working at the reception area directly in front of the door, felt the heat shrivel her patience like a raisin.

Through the large picture window, she saw a car pull onto the visitor's lot. It was just a blur until she put her glasses back on. A figure bolted from the driver's seat and slammed the door of the weathered auto. Christy put up her guard as a shabbily dressed civilian hot-footed it across the lot and headed toward the entrance. There was something familiar about his gait.

He pushed open the door and said the phrase everyone was sick of hearing: "Hot enough for ya?"

She stared at the figure in the doorway and tried to find something familiar under the bushy beard and lank hair. The voice was teasing and packed too many memories. "Wolfe?"

He reached up, hooked a finger through the bridge of his sunglasses, and pulled them down, revealing green eyes. James Wolfe, AKA Wolfe, AKA Wolfman.

"What are you doing here?" she demanded.

He feigned hurt, pouting his lower lip. "I thought you'd be a happy to see me."

"Oh, yeah, I'm just jumping for joy."

Christy had seen the new roster and knew Wolfe was now assigned to the undercover narcotics unit. Still, nothing prepared her for his transformation. The clean-cut deputy, once all spit and polish in uniform, was gone. The man who stood before her looked like a dope addict on a bad day.

"Who are you here to see?" she asked coldly.

"Actually," Wolfe drawled, looking down the empty corridor, "I'm here to see you. I was hoping to get you alone."

"We are alone."

He leaned over the counter and smiled at her. "Aw, don't be like that. I need a little favor."

Six months after their break-up and here he was again, trying to wheedle something out of her. Just when she was getting over feeling used.

"Is this business?"

"Something like that."

Christy turned her head to look at the computer screen and resumed typing. "I'm sure you have secretaries over at the narc unit to take care of you."

"Not for this. I need you to do a horoscope for me."

He was the last person she'd expect to hear mouth those words. He had no way of knowing she still kept an astrology chart on him. Sagittarius. Mercury rising. At one time, she'd checked it every couple of weeks, astrologically spying on him. Now, she even didn't bother to with updates.

"Oh, like you ever believed in astrology. What did you call it? My 'horrible scopes.'"

"I still don't buy into that crap," Wolfe said, "but I know someone who does."

"Not interested."

Footsteps were heard coming down the hall. Wolfe leaned over the counter and grabbed her arm. "You'll be interested after I tell you the details. Meet me on the patio out back." He bolted out the front door.

Christy could still feel the heat from his hand on her skin when Lennie Watkins turned the corner. She was fanning herself with a handful of forms. "That wasn't Deputy Perez who just left, was it? He didn't fill out his stat sheet, and the sergeant is in his office having a fit. I don't need that man to go cardiac on me."

Christy stared at the front door. Decision time.

"Lennie, can you watch the front desk for ten minutes? I've got to take care of a problem."

ɛɔɛɔ

The small patio was an island of concrete surrounded by a cyclone fence. Wild sunflowers clung to the wires and made a yellow barrier between the substation and the grape fields. The aluminum tables, hot as griddles, received scant shade by flimsy umbrellas. Wolfe sat under one of them, sweating. When he saw her, he patted the seat next to him. Instead, she took a seat across the table. She needed some distance between them.

Christy looked around to see if any deputies were watching. She straightened an imaginary crease in her pants. "This better be good," she muttered.

"Just hear me out."

He ran his fingers through the thatch of hair on his chin, probably expecting her to comment on his new look. With the sun to his back, he was all shadow and silhouette. "I've been working some major cases in Narcotics these days. Maybe you heard?"

Christy shrugged. "I heard you went undercover. Looks like the rumors were true."

Wolfe looked down at his ripped Levis and dirty tank top and grinned. "Gotta dress the part." Then he put on his serious face. "Here's the deal. I've got an investigation going on a methamphetamine dealer who has a network of distributors all over the valley. We busted two of his runners, but they don't know where the lab is located."

Christy held up her hand to stop the flow of details. "Way too much information. Isn't what you do confidential?"

"Confidential to the public, but come on. You've

worked at the sheriff's department for eight years. I know I can trust you."

"Just like I thought I could trust you?"

Wolfe pinched his lips together in a tight line. She wished she could see his eyes behind those damn sunglasses.

"The past is what it is, I can't change anything. I'm asking you to hear me out." The tone of his voice said it was no fair mixing the past with serious business. Work always came first. "The man I'm talking about is Lloyd Parr. Word on the street is that he not only manufactures meth, but anyone who gets on his bad side winds up dead. We can't pin anything on him because he's got men who do his dirty work for him. They're called the Black Hearts."

"The motorcycle gang." Christy flashed back to numerous "Disturbing the Peace" reports that had come across her desk. The Black Hearts were regulars.

"Former motorcycle gang. Parr took them off their Harleys a few years back and put them to work cooking crank in area of Rialto. It's a tough group to infiltrate, but I was getting close."

Christy looked past him out over the field, her eyes squinting against the blistering sun as she absorbed the information. She wished she'd brought along her sunglasses.

"This is fascinating, Wolfe, but it's hot out here and

I've got to get back to work. My break's over. Lennie will be sending out a search party soon."

Wolfe picked up the pace. "Here's the deal. I subpoenaed Parr's phone records and found out he was making one-nine-hundred calls to an astrology hotline. I'm talking two to three hundred dollars a month. This guy is hooked on Dial-A-Horoscope."

That hit a nerve." Those readings are so generic. How could anybody believe in that stuff?"

"Astrology, tarot cards, crystal balls, it's all bunk. People are gullible. You should know that."

Amazing. Wolfe was baiting her and asking for her help at the same time. He was too wrapped up in his story to see the irony of the situation.

"It doesn't matter what I believe," he continued. "If Parr wants to be guided by the stars, then I'll give him a map that leads right to prison. Here's how you're gonna help me. I want you to do Parr's horoscope."

He said it like he'd just handed her a gift and was expecting a thank-you note.

To Christy, it was a slap in the face.

He was asking—no, he was ordering, browbeating, and shaming her—into performing the very act that caused them to split up.

At the beginning of their relationship astrology wasn't an issue because Christy never told him she cast horoscopes. He found out after he moved in with her and caught her pouring over charts and jotting down strange symbols. At first, he thought it was "cute," and "quirky." He made jokes about living with a witch. Some women quilted, some women made artsy-crafty do-dads. His girl-friend told the future.

He was a little unnerved when she predicted the out-come of cases he had to testify on in court. He went along when she scheduled their vacations based on positive planetary alignments ("Honey, let's wait for Jupiter to reach the ninth house before we go to San Diego.") At some point…was it in the second year?…her "gift" be-came stronger and his tolerance lessened.

Then it got ugly. She would offer suggestions for small decisions in his life, just a nudge in the direction the stars were pointing. He reacted by doing the exact opposite. The planets weren't the only things in opposi-tion. Their whole universe was in conflict.

Saturn moved into the fifth house. Wolfe packed up and moved out.

And now he was back, asking for a favor in the rud-est way possible. Insult to injury.

Christy stood up. "It's not going to happen." She started past him, but he grabbed her arm.

It stopped her. Not just because his grip was enough to leave bruises. She was picking up a rush of feelings, premonitions, energy transferred from Wolfe's body into hers.

Damn, she hated when that happened.

She pried his fingers off her arm and sat down on the bench next to him. "Why is this so important to you? I want to know everything, not the *Reader's Digest* version."

Wolfe wiped his forehead with the bottom of his shirt. "I think he killed a snitch I was using. The kid's street name was Johnny Blue. We got Blue into the Black Heart's inner circle after months of making buys. A week ago, he disappeared."

"If you think he was murdered, why aren't you talking to Homicide?"

"Without a body? Naw, Homicide won't bother with a missing snitch. Everyone figures he just turned tail and headed south. But I've been working with this informant. He's not in it for the money. His sister ran with the gang for a while and got messed up on drugs. It's personal."

Christy shook her head. "I'm still not following you. You want me to do this drug dealer's horoscope because..."

"I think I can hink him up pretty bad. See, all I'm asking you to do is dummy up a horoscope and throw in all sorts of crazy warnings from the grave, or the stars, whatever. If I can get it to him, maybe it'll lure him out and he'll lead us to the body. We might finally put him behind bars for life."

But Christy was riveted on only one line in the sentence. "I don't do phony horoscopes. If you're asking me to alter this guy's chart to suit your purposes, just forget it."

"What's your damn problem?"

"I'm a good astrologer, whether you believe it or not. My credibility is involved here. You wouldn't know much about that."

"No, I'm too busy dealing with murder."

Christy couldn't top that one, so she changed tactics. "What does your sergeant think about your plan?"

Wolfe put his head down and shifted uncomfortably. She didn't need to see his eyes.

"You didn't clear this with the sergeant, did you?" What a surprise. "This whole scheme of yours reeks of entrapment. Let's say I did the damn horoscope, and you managed to pull it off. What are you going to do—put me on the witness stand to testify? An astrology defense isn't going to fly. You'd go down in flames, Lloyd Parr would walk." She stood up again. "Find someone else to do your dirty work."

"Oh, like I know any other astrologers. And even if I did, you're the only one I could trust."

Now he was resorting to flattery. Nothing had changed between them.

"What you're asking me to do could get us both in big trouble." She walked past him

Wolfe reached out and grabbed her wrist. There was

that heat again, rushing up her arm and scrambling her brain.

"Why are you so afraid to take chances?" he chided. "Oh, I know you're Miss By-the-Book, but sometimes you gotta toss the book out. And this is one of those times, Christy. Lloyd Parr doesn't play by the rules. Why should we?"

She jerked her arm out of his grasp. "You're the risk taker, Wolfe. You get paid to stick your neck out. All I do is file papers in an office. You're not talking me into getting involved."

"How can you work in law enforcement and not be involved? You're part of this. I'm just asking you to do what you're good at. Come on, Christy. Give me the horoscope. Nobody has to know where it came from."

She eyed him warily. "Will it really make that big of a difference to the case?"

"We'll never know unless we try. It could change a lot of lives. Maybe even save one."

It was so like Wolfe to throw down a dare. His proposal was too much to process, especially with the sun frying her brain. "I'll think about it. That's all I can give you for now."

"I'll take it."

Wolfe stood up and moved in, clearly expecting a hug to seal the deal. He smelled bad and looked worse. Christy ducked out of reach and trotted back to the safety of the office. She hoped no one was staring through the tinted windows.

CHAPTER 3

After Wolfe left, Christy went back inside to the welcomed relief of the air conditioner. She hurried past the front desk, but not fast enough.

"Where are you going?" Lennie said. "You had a break."

"I have to run some names. Can you handle the phones a little while longer? This won't take more than a few minutes."

Christy sat down in front of an ancient computer terminal and logged on. There was no mouse, every command was done by key stroke. It took three punches on the stubborn message key before it accepted her entry code. She settled back in the chair and watched the cursor do a slow glide over the screen, line by invisible line.

Department computers weren't for personal use, a rule Christy normally adhered to. Technically, what she was about to do was law enforcement related. Not authorized, but related. It made her uncomfortable to cross the fine line, but right now her curiosity was strong enough to bend the rules. She typed in the name. The screen flickered.

Lloyd Parr. White male adult, five foot ten, one hundred eighty pounds, brown hair, hazel eyes. Identifiable marks: a tattoo of a shark on his chest. Christy noted a few warrants for minor infractions, none of them active. No recent jail time. If Parr was as bad as Wolfe said, it sure didn't show on his county rap sheet. She weighed the pros and cons of running a criminal history check through the state-wide system. There was a chance that the file was flagged, and the last thing she needed in her life were state investigators calling the sheriff and asking about her interest in Parr.

As she studied the keyboard, wondering what to run next, Christy flashed onto one of her father's tried and true sayings: "If you want to know a man, know his friends and enemies." She rapidly typed "Asso," the access code to the Associates File (dubbed the Asshole File), followed by Parr's six-digit designator. Five names popped up: Joseph Youngblood, Sr.; Joseph Youngblood, Jr.; Trace Malin; Tim Neeley; and Alex Trimmer. Birds of a feather.

The file on the elder Youngblood covered several screens, and although Christy was tempted to pull them up, she knew she would not have time to look them over. Information was sketchy on Trimmer and Neeley.

Joey, Jr. and Malin were familiar names from the reports she filed. Joey was in and out of trouble, first as a juvenile offender, then graduating into petty crime. He appeared to be following in the footsteps of his father.

Trace Malin was a small-time dealer who sold marijuana out of an auto wrecking yard. The deputies tagged him "Without a Trace" Malin, although he was usually without a clue when he solicited undercover narcs for a joint or two. He seemed to have disappeared from the area, although word had it that he'd moved to Eugene, Oregon, to become a pot farmer.

Reluctant to be caught printing out the information, Christy studied the screen and committed as much info as she could to memory before pressing the clear button. The data disappeared.

She went into the break room to see what was left in the snack machine. Whatever it held would be lunch. Sergeant Traynor sat at the Formica table, looking over reports with an ever-present mug of coffee in hand.

"How's it going, Christy."

"Hey, Sarge."

"They haven't refilled the machine yet. Don't get the chips. They're stale." He tossed an empty carton of yogurt in the trash and pulled out a few carrots from his lunch sack. Since his divorce, he'd been trying to get his weight down before getting back into the dating scene. Rumor had it that he had his eye on a divorcee working in Records.

Traynor always looked out for Lennie and her. He had weathered the administration of five sheriffs in his career and lived by the motto inscribed on the side of his patrol car, *To Protect and To Serve*. He'd never been able to pass the test for lieutenant, but trained the younger deputies for the job. His value as a field sergeant was never disputed. He knew every inch of the county he patrolled. He was sure to have more information than the computer data base.

As she slipped coins into the soda machine and punched the tab for Dr Pepper, she casually asked "Sarge, does the name Joseph Youngblood ring a bell?"

"Junior or Senior?"

"I guess you just answered my question."

"Youngblood, Sr. is an old crankster," Sergeant Traynor replied, using the slang for meth users. "Used to run with a motorcycle gang that had an insignia of a playing card on the back of their leathers, the seven of hearts. Called themselves Black Hearts. Why do you ask? Was a report filed recently?"

"No, just curious. His name came up when the guys were talking about old cases. I figured you'd know more than any of them."

It was almost too easy to get Traynor talking.

"Youngblood Senior, or 'Blood,' as we used to call him, was the cooker. He set up labs all over the county, hid them so well that all we ever found was the mess they left for us to clean up."

Christy sipped her soda. "Sounds like a colorful group."

"Oh, yeah, they were, in their heyday. We nabbed a few minor players and put them away. Never could get their leader, a low-life by the name of Lloyd Parr. He managed to stay one step ahead of us. There were rumors floating around that he put contracts out on people who crossed him. A few bodies showed up, but no proof ever linked him to the murders. Scum killing scum, not worth an investigation."

Traynor stood up and crushed the aluminum can in one huge hand. He tossed it in the recycle bin and headed to his office.

Time to relieve Lennie. Christy walked back to her station feeling a little guilty about peeking into Parr's computer records. But it wasn't like she'd done something illegal.

Not yet, anyway.

CHAPTER 4

W hat was going on today? You didn't even eat lunch." Lennie folded her five-foot-eleven-inch frame into the driver's seat of the Volvo and turned the ignition key. The engine caught after three tries.

"Did you see me with out on the patio with a nasty looking guy?"

Lennie nodded. She didn't miss much around the office.

"That was my ex."

"I thought you had better taste." Lennie held up her hand. "He's undercover. I get it. I saw the roster too. Why did he come sniffing around?"

Christy let the rush of hot air from the open windows drown out her roommate's question. The Volvo's air conditioner only seem to work in the dead of winter.

The first six months without Wolfe were the hardest. The deputies kept their distance, gauging her reaction to the break-up, supporting Wolfe's decision with their silence. She found herself undatable, an outcast because of some unspoken code the men in department followed. It was irritating and devastating at the same time.

Lennie was new to the department, fresh off a ranch in Riverton and recovering from a nasty divorce. Christy soon discovered her co-worker had never touched a computer in her life, a fact the county overlooked when they offered her the position at the substation. Training Lennie became a full-time job and took Christy's mind off Wolfe for eight hours a day.

Misery loved company, and Lennie desperately needed a place closer to work than her apartment in Kearny. With more than a few misgivings, Christy offered her co-worker the extra room in her Victorian apartment on the outskirts of Coronita. There seemed to be too much extra space after Wolfe moved his things out.

Christy felt a nudge at her leg.

"I said, what did he want?" Lennie shouted over the wind and Garth Brooks.

"He wants me to do a horoscope."

"Thought you said he was a non-believer."

"It's for a…friend."

They were entering the city limits of Coronita, population eight thousand. "The Crown of Central County" according to the logo on the Rotary Club sign. Lennie slowed to twenty-five miles an hour and coasted down Muscat Boulevard, past the business district of modern stores housed in turn-of-the-century buildings. Even in the late afternoon heat, people were power-walking under the lush shade of poplars and catching their breath on cool marble benches. A group of young mothers gossiped as their kids splashed in the five-sided fountain in the park. A few recognized the Volvo and gave a friendly wave.

Coronita was different from other satellite towns that revolved around the center hub of Kearny. The community held on to its individualism and a way of life that was slower, more aesthetic than the surrounding farm communities. Bookstores outnumbered fast food chains, and a first edition Saroyan or an autographed Steinbeck was easier to come by than a Whopper with all the trimmings. It was a little bit of Berkeley in the San Joaquin Valley.

Christy's neighbors were artists, writers, aging hippies, New Age believers, university professors, and people escaping Kearny's big-city growth. When she made it known that she did astrology, nobody raised a cultured eyebrow.

Small town coziness and culture aside, the main attraction of Coronita for Christy and Lennie was the close proximity to the substation. Lennie's Volvo limped along on its last Swedish leg, and Christy's Fiat spent more time in the shop than in the driveway. When both cars were out of commission, they called Sergeant Traynor, who dispatched a deputy to taxi them to work. Lennie swung the car into the circular driveway of a yellow gingerbread Victorian. The owner, Mrs. Alcorn, occupied the ground level apartment. Hard of hearing and half blind, she remained oblivious to their comings and goings or Lennie's loud music. Unfortunately, this wasn't the case with Jonathan Maciel, who lived in the attic apartment, wore bow ties and berets, and narrowed his eyes whenever he spotted the women. Even on scorching hot days like today, they used the outdoor stairway at the rear to avoid running into him. Lennie's long legs mounted the stairs two at a time and Christy followed more slowly, puffing to catch up.

No matter how rough the day, Christy looked forward to fitting the key in the lock and being greeted by light streaming through tall, curtainless windows. They couldn't afford drapes, but three ficus trees and two potted palms acted as curtains and gave a greenhouse effect. The rest of the apartment appeared spacious because neither woman owned much in the way of furniture. All of Lennie's household goods were held hostage in the hands of her ex. She'd fled the marriage with just the clothes she could stuff into a suitcase and a hundred-year-old milk pitcher handed down by Great-Grandmother Dobbs.

Christy's father was a civilian who worked with the air force, so the family moved every few years. Her mother found it easier to shop than pack. Always surrounded by new things, Christy learned not to get attached to possessions or people. She furnished the apartment economically with cast-offs from friends and flea market treasures. Every few months her mother offered credit cards and years of experience to entice her to redecorate. But Christy found she liked furniture that had a history—even if it wasn't her own.

She went into the bedroom and shucked her wilted clothes. She pulled a muu muu out of the closet and slipped it over her head. The cotton felt blessedly cool against her skin. As she pinned her damp hair up off her neck, her eyes were drawn to the reflection of the brass bed in the cracked vanity mirror.

It wasn't really brass, just iron with many coats of spray paint. Wolfe had hated the bed, hated the way the mattress lumped and the springs squealed. He said it broke his concentration. Now the paint needed a touch-up, gray metal was showing through, and with the weight of one body, the coils barely made a sound. *Don't do this,* she scolded. She wiped an imaginary smudge off the mirror with her thumb and left the room.

Pushing away thoughts of next month's electrical bill, Christy flicked on the air conditioner and tugged the pull-cords of the ceiling fans in the kitchen and living room for good measure. Lennie was already pouring raspberry herbal tea in glasses filled with ice.

Christy's routine was the always the same: tea, the newspaper, and total silence while the stress of the day dissolved. Today she went right to the bookcase and pulled several volumes of astrology off the shelf. She carried the books and the glass of tea over to the couch and sank into its faded chintz roses.

"You haven't cast a horoscope in about three months," Lennie said, putting a coaster under the glass.

"No, and I haven't decided if I'm going to do this one yet."

If she got as far as constructing the horoscope wheel, Christy knew she'd be drawn into the chart. All the pieces would come together, creating patterns from the patchwork of planets, signs, and houses. It didn't matter how many times she drew the circle or how much time had passed, the force of the horoscope always amazed her. She learned early not to resist, to follow the course and be a guide for others.

Lennie sat down across from her in the Bentwood rocker and ran a finger round the rim of her glass. "By the way, when am I supposed to come into the money you keep seeing in my chart?"

"Lennie, I don't have time right now."

"Just refresh my memory, and I promise I'll leave you alone."

Christy took off her glasses and rubbed her weary eyes. "When Neptune enters your eighth house. Somebody dies. It could happen anytime in the next three years."

"I wish the stars would be more specific. I could use the money right now."

"Couldn't we all." Slipping her glasses back on, Christy turned her attention to the books.

They were all spread before her on the marble coffee table, but she automatically reached for the battered blue volume by Alexis Park. The dust jacket was faded and there were stains on the binding. The well-thumbed book functioned as her primer, the basis for all her horoscopes. Thirteen years ago it caught her eye through the dirty panes of a used bookstore in Kearny's Tower District. It cost twelve dollars, a fortune in those days. The store's owner looked at her curiously when he retrieved it from the display and blew the dust off.

"Are you an astrologer?" he'd asked, and she'd said no, but at once felt guilty, as if she'd told a lie. In the end, he let her have it for eight dollars.

Psychic ability ran in her family, but she'd stubbornly resisted urges she didn't want to understand, until the day she held that dusty volume. When she opened the book of strange yet oddly familiar symbols, Christy realized she closed the chapters of denial in her life.

It was her secret, especially after she began working

in law enforcement. But she found herself charting friends, to help them through rough times, and friends of friends until her reputation grew. Finally, after clearing it with Vice, she began charging a small fee for the charts she made. Lennie came up with the idea of posting flyers around town and registering with The Crystal Orb, the only occult shop in Kearny. The deputies kidded her for weeks and called her "Madame Christy," but nobody in the sheriff's department took her seriously. Especially Wolfe.

Christy opened the ephemeris to Lloyd Parr's birth date. It wouldn't hurt to take a peek into this man's chart, but that's as far as she'd go. She drew a circle and intersected it with six lines until it looked like a pie sliced into twelve pieces. Each portion was thirty degrees. Referencing a table listing the sign and degree, Christy placed the symbol of each planet at the designated location on the wheel.

Without going any further, Christy knew she was looking at the natal chart of a dangerous man. More dangerous than Wolfe realized. Then she felt the threat reach off the page and out to her.

CHAPTER 5

"Y"ou finished it?" Wolfe kept his eager voice at low volume over the phone. Christy heard the bantering of other narcs in the background.

"Yes. It's a rush job, but it's done." She kept her own voice low.

"Meet me at the Shanghai when you get off. We'll have dinner while I look it over."

"You'll have to pick me up. My car's in the shop again."

Lennie rounded the corner like a bloodhound following a scent. She instantly picked up the whiff of a date.

"Don't tell me you're still driving the same green Fiat?" Wolfe lectured. "It should have been in the junkyard five years ago. Stop pouring money into that heap and buy a decent car."

"If I made your salary, I'd buy a Porsche. Give me

twenty bucks for the horoscope so I can start saving up."

"Never mind. I'll pick you up at the office. Five o'clock. Be ready."

"Got a date with Wolfe, huh?" Lennie passed Christy a Diet Dr Pepper. "Is there something going on I should know about?"

Christy popped open her soda. "It's purely business."

"There's nothing pure in this business."

Christy riffled through the afternoon's work piled up on the desk. "You're right. Murder, mayhem, molestation. Take your pick." Christy plucked a report off her desk. "PC 647a, Indecent Exposure. One of my all-time favorites."

"Here, let me look at that wienie-wagger so I don't wind up on a blind date with him." Lennie plucked the report off Christy's desk and started reading the good parts.

"So, roommate," Lennie said casually without looking up from the file, "why is the big bad Wolfe visiting our end of the forest again?"

"It's narc business." Christy busied herself with the report form in front of her. "Like they say, `If I tell you, I'd have to kill you.'"

Lennie put the report down. "Oh? Well, last time I checked, you weren't working undercover. And I sure didn't see any openings for Narcotics Secretary posted on the bulletin board. I'll bet this has something to do with that horoscope the other night."

Christy felt her ears turning red. "I'm giving him an unofficial assist, so don't say anything, okay?"

"Christy, I don't know what the hell's going on, so what could I say and who would I say it to?" Lennie's hazel eyes scrutinized her friend. "Is it legal?"

"I hope so." Christy shifted uncomfortably. "Wolfe's picking me up after work. I should be home around nine."

"You haven't forgotten he's married, have you?"

"It's strictly business. When it's all over, I'll tell you every detail. I promise. Now, let me get some work done."

"Fat chance. The computers have been down for forty-five minutes." Lennie slid off the desk and picked up the empty soda cans. On the way to the recycling bin, she stopped at the door and turned to Christy. "I expect you to keep your promises."

☙❧

Wolfe pulled in twenty minutes late, spewing gravel with his entrance. The LTD, new in the mid-seventies and now looking worse for wear, was Wolfe's undercover vehicle of choice. Unofficially dubbed the "Crankmobile," all attempts to retire the gas-guzzler met with staunch opposition by Wolfe, who was convinced that his successful drug buying stemmed from the seedy appearance of his car. The Crankmobile and its driver were inseparable.

In torn levis, armless fatigue shirt, and baseball cap with a marijuana leaf insignia, Detective Wolfe looked like the street scum the deputies usually arrested. Older deputies leaned on their patrol cars and gave him a half-lidded look, accompanied by a slight nod. There was a coolness between Patrol and Detective Division, known by their call sign as the Adam units. Among themselves, the deputies referred to the narcs as "Two Adam Too Good." But, given the opportunity, many of the younger deputies would jump at the chance to grow their hair long, wear grungy clothes, and pass themselves off as drug dealers.

Christy bolted out the front door and kept her red-dened face pointed at the pavement. Damn Wolfe! Because he was late, the deputies were already out of briefing. They stared as their office assistant climbed into the Crankmobile. She could feel her reputation plummet as Wolfe hit the gas pedal and shot out of the lot.

Christy turned to look back at the parking lot, only to find herself staring at five black balloons bobbing in the back seat.

"What's with the balloons?" she asked. "It's not my birthday."

"It's part of my plan," Wolfe replied with a grin. "I'll tell you about it after dinner."

The Shanghai Express had the distinction of being the only Chinese restaurant in Coronita, but it did little to capitalize on this fact. The windows were clouded with an accumulation of grease and grime, and narrow slits marred the red plastic upholstery. The restaurant did a brisk business for a Tuesday, and the foyer overflowed with customers waiting for take-out. Wolfe and Christy slipped into the main dining area and headed for their favorite booth.

A waitress slammed two acrylic tumblers of ice water on the table, then shoved a pair of stained menus into their hands, and disappeared. "Nothing's changed around here." Wolfe sighed. "I haven't had Chinese food in a long time."

"You used to live on the stuff. What happened?"

"The wife prefers Thai."

Christy bent her head and concentrated on the selections in front of her. Wolfe reached over and took the menu out of her hands.

"Why bother reading it? You always order the same thing—broccoli chicken on rice, not noodles."

The restaurant suddenly felt too warm. Her glasses fogged.

"Am I that predictable?"

"I've never seen you order anything else here. Face it, Christy, you've always resisted change. You haven't changed your hairstyle since I've known you. And you still wear shapeless tops to cover your body." He reached across the table, slipped her glasses off her face and polished them with a napkin. "You won't even try contacts. I think you're afraid to let people see your incredible eyes."

Talking about her eyes made her lower them. They were the palest blue, fading to nearly white sometimes. People used to stop in their tracks at her gaze before she started wearing glasses. She found lightly tinted lenses toned down the effect and made her feel normal.

Plunking a chipped teapot on the table, the waitress waited for their order. Christy snatched her glasses and put them on as Wolfe ordered the sparerib combination plate and a large Pepsi. The waitress turned to Christy. "I'll have tangerine beef with noodles, egg foo yung, and two egg rolls a la carte."

Wolfe waited until the waitress left, then fished his wallet out, and checked his funds. "Are you trying to break me?"

"Be glad I didn't order the lobster."

The food arrived. Wolfe pushed his fork aside and picked up the chopsticks. Leave it to him to do things the hard way. Her eyes wandered as she nibbled on tangerine rind, wishing it was broccoli. Wolfe was right. The Shanghai hadn't changed over the years. Red plaster dragons still decorated the walls and the waitresses were still rude. The only thing different was their relationship.

She looked at Wolfe balancing a rib between the chopsticks. He wore his thinning hair pulled back in a lank ponytail, and he had more forehead then she remembered. Crow's feet etched the corners of his eyes, and gray weaved through his trailing beard. Maybe she looked the same, but change didn't flatter him at all.

"You're picking at your food. Don't you like it?" Switching to a fork, he reached across the table and snagged an egg roll. He always sampled off her plate, even when they ordered the same dish. It still irritated her. He took a generous portion of the beef and half of her egg foo yung without offering anything in return.

"So, let's have a look at Parr's chart. I hope this horoscope is worth the price of the meal you're eating."

Christy passed him the manila envelope and watched as he read, his lips moving slightly as he worked his way through the astrological jargon. Finally, he put the pages down.

"This is his real horoscope? You didn't doctor it up?"

"I told you I wasn't going to fake it." Christy poured green tea into a thimble-size teacup, emptied a packet of sugar into it, and stirred with the wrong end of her fork. "He's dangerous, isn't he? Saturn is moving into the second house, and that's putting him under pressure. And Mars indicates trouble with men, either other drug dealers, or maybe it means the narc team. He's not stable right now. He's like a bomb, wired to go off at any second."

Wolfe stared at her intently as she talked, his fingers pulling at his wiry mustache. "You've gotten inside info written in here that I never told you. Have you talked to anyone else about this case?"

She stopped stirring. "I pumped Sergeant Traynor for background on the Youngbloods. I never mentioned Parr."

"Well, you've nailed him on paper. I don't know where you came up with some of this stuff. It's eerie."

She sipped the tea. It was sweet and soothing. "I thought you didn't believe in any of this."

"I don't. But I believe in you. And I think this horoscope is pretty convincing."

The waitress brought the check and two fortune cookies. Wolfe's hand wavered over them, trying to decide which one was his. Finally, he chose one and cracked it open like an egg.

"'Many paths lead to the same destination.' What the hell does that mean?"

Christy ignored him, transfixed by the slip of paper in her hand. "A wise river divides around the rock."

"Are you going to eat your cookie?" Wolfe asked as he snatched it up. He stood and fished a few crumbled bills out of his pocket.

Christy continued to stare at the piece of paper. She didn't move until Wolfe asked if she could cover the tip. When she reached for her wallet, she slipped the fortune into the side pocket of her purse.

CHAPTER 6

They left the Shanghai and walked to the car. Once in the Crankmobile, Wolfe headed to the outskirts of town.

"I guess you forgot where I live," Christy said.

"You're still in our old apartment on Raisin Ridge, aren't you? How could I forget that place?" He cracked the window and picked up speed as they left Coronita. "It's a nice night, we've just had a good meal. I thought we'd take a drive in the country."

Why was she sitting next to him hurling down county back roads at breakneck speed, black balloons riding shotgun? Because he needed more than the horoscope. She realized he needed a confidante. The whole scheme had to stay under wraps since using astrology to catch a crook would probably land him smack in the middle of Internal Affairs. Wolfe didn't play by the rules, he never had, but now he expected her to break those rules with him.

"Tell me you're not enjoying this."

Christy turned away and watched the farmland flow by. She silently admitted that some part of her was enjoying the drama and the intoxication of being with Wolfe again. But she was also angry. How typical of Wolfe to abduct her for the night, without asking if she had other plans. He assumed she would be there for him. Frustrated, she settled back into the car's upholstery.

But he was right. It was a beautiful July night. Lights from farmhouses dotted the countryside and row upon row of grapevines gave way to orchards of peaches, plums and Fuji apples. Despite her lousy sense of direction, she deduced by the shift in crops that they were headed toward the south end of Central County. The night had cooled to the mid-eighties and she closed her eyes and savored the hot ripple of air as they cruised.

"This reminds me of the ride-alongs that I coaxed you on when I was in Patrol." His voice was quiet. Summer-night memories were also stirring in him. "Remember the drive to Coalton and that arson call we rolled Code Three on?"

"The air smelled like cantaloupe and the fire was out before we got there."

"Yeah, that's right." He paused to savor the memory. "We had some good times. What happened?"

"You got married."

She didn't mean for it to come out so accusatory. She didn't mean to say it at all. But there it was, dropped in the space between them like a cold egg roll.

They rode in embarrassed silence for several miles before his foot eased on the accelerator. "I know I owe you an explanation. I always meant to talk to you about it. See? I liked living with you, but I didn't think it was a good idea to get too serious. There's a saying in the locker room: 'You don't piss where you eat.' I wanted a wife with no ties to law enforcement. You can understand that, can't you?"

"Get off it, Wolfe. Lots of deputies marry dispatchers, captains marry their secretaries. Even Sheriff Nolan married an ID tech." She tried not to sound defensive.

"Those are second marriages, the one you marry after you realize what they say in the locker room is bullshit. After you catch on that the woman working next to you eight hours a day understands you better than your wife."

For weeks after he packed up and moved out and the sergeant posted his transfer on the bulletin board, Christy scoured her mind to find a reason for Wolfe's desertion. His timing was terrible, less than a month after she turned thirty. Suddenly, there appeared gray at her temples and fine lines at the corners of her eyes. She never seriously thought about marrying Wolfe, but once he closed the door to the apartment and her options, panic set in. The first tick of her biological clock echoed in the emptiness. Real pain came seven months later when Wolfe passed out wedding invitations. She tore hers up and fed it to the shredder.

"Melissa—" He glanced over to see the effect his wife's name had Christy. "—is a pediatric nurse. She always comes home and talks about sick babies, which bores the shit out of me. I can't tell her anything about my work, but what I do on the street scares her. If she had her way, I'd be back in a patrol car. She bitches that she married a man who shaved every day and wore a clean uniform, not a ratty dope dealer. You know how much I love being a narc, Christy. I worked hard to get this assignment. But my wife doesn't accept it. She won't get near me anymore."

Melissa had a point. It was hard to look at Wolfe and not label him undesirable. Even walking into the Shanghai, Christy felt eyes asking "What's a nice girl like you doing with someone like him?" But over tea and chow mein, she got past the ponytail and scraggly beard, and he was Wolfe again. Sexy, green-eyed Wolfe. Now an unhappily married man.

Suddenly, the night felt much too nostalgic. "We'd better get back. It's late and I have to be at my desk by eight sharp."

"Don't worry, I'll have you in bed by ten. Anyway we're almost there."

Wolfe slowed the Crankmobile and turned off the lights. They coasted in semi-darkness. Ten-foot-high oleander bushes formed a barricade between the road and a house recessed into the grape fields.

A chill took hold of Christy and her throat tightened as though an invisible hand gripped it. She knew the answer but she asked the question anyway. "Where are we?"

"Parr's house."

It was the same feeling of dread which reached out from the horoscope, only ten times stronger.

"We have to get out of here, Wolfe. Now."

"First, we deliver the horoscope." Wolfe picked up the manila folder and passed it to her. "Get out of the car and slip this in his mailbox."

She sat paralyzed.

"Go on, Christy. It'll just take a second."

She looked into Wolfe's glittering eyes and taut smile. The danger of being so close to Parr excited him. He was like a small boy teasing a pit bull on a short chain.

She shoved the envelope back at him. "You do it."

"I have to be ready to hit the gas in case one of the guards spots us. That's why I brought you along." His hairy arm reached across her and tugged on the handle until the door opened, then he punched the button on her safety belt. It snapped across her lap and into its holster.

"Go on." He prodded her shoulder. "It'll only take a second. The longer we sit here, the more attention we'll attract."

Christy reluctantly got out of the car.

A rusted mailbox tilted on a wood post in front of her. Beside it perched an orange plastic tube with *Kearny Sun* printed in black letters. The cracked tube angled toward the ground where a small pile of newspapers rotted.

The hinges of the mailbox squealed in protest as she tugged open the mouth. The sound screamed in the still night and grated her raw nerves. There was mail in the box, old mail shoved in the back, crumpled. Christy folded the manila envelope in half and frantically crammed it in the remaining space. She bolted for the car and tugged at the door.

Wolfe reached across the seat to thrust the string of balloons at her. "Go back and tie these on to the flag."

"What?"

"Tie the balloons to the metal arm of the mailbox up so Parr will check it out."

"Go to hell. You let me back in this car." She fought the bobbing balloons which were escaping out the door. Finally, she gave up and grabbed the string.

Retracing her steps, she groped in the dark and searched for the flag. She wound the string around the rusted metal, tugged to make sure it held, and raced back to the car.

She leapt into the passenger seat, and Wolfe cautioned her not to slam the door. As she reached for the seatbelt, he put two fingers under her chin and turned her head toward him. She slapped his hand away.

"I don't need your kisses. Just get me out of here."

Pluto seeks to change existing conditions through upheaval or chaos.

CHAPTER 7

The voice over the phone sounded tentative, a tone of reluctance tempered by curiosity. Christy had received several calls during the week, all responding to her recent ad in the Coronita supermarket flyer. Some were chatty, most were nervous, and none turned into clients.

Christy made her voice as reassuring as possible. "What's your date and time of birth?"

The woman rattled off the information, hesitating briefly before confessing the year.

"Do you want me to chart your natal horoscope, your future, or both?"

"You can tell my future?"

"I can tell you what the stars and planets are doing in your future." She used Wolfe's analogy. "It's like reading a map—the chart points you in the right direction, but you chose the road."

"Just a minute, okay?" On the other end, a hand cupped the mouthpiece and two muffled voices filtered through. "But she can tell my future!" whined the female voice.

Christy doodled on a notepad as she waited for the outcome. Her artistic ability was limited to stick figures, but she sketched a sunrise between two palm trees. Maybe it was a sunset. She wrote "Natal Only" next to Emilina Perez's name as the argument on the other end heated up. It didn't take a psychic to know the man was winning.

"Just a plain horoscope," the woman sulked. "How much?"

Christy quoted her usual fee of thirty-five dollars and instructed the woman to send the check to the Raisin Ridge address.

"Do you want to meet with me when the chart's ready? You might have some questions," Christy asked.

Another conference took place off the line. Christy felt her patience growing thinner every time she was put on hold.

"Send it to this, uh, post office box." Emilina stumbled over the numbers of a PO box located in the town of Rialto. It didn't sound like a mailing address the woman was familiar with.

"It'll take me about a week—"

"Okay."

There was no goodbye, just a dial tone.

Christy stared at the receiver in her hand before hanging up. She slowly tore the page off the notepad. Lennie, who was spending the Saturday morning sprawled on the couch with a stack of back issues of Cosmopolitan, looked up from her reading. "Another new client, Ms. Stargazer?"

"Um-hmm." Christy studied Emilina Perez's birth date. "The woman was being coached. A man in the background told her exactly what to say."

"Maybe the horoscope's really for him. Would you be able to tell if someone was giving you another person's birth date?"

Good question. When she did horoscopes for free, people often tested her abilities with bad information. It cost her in man-hours and mental strain to sort through the unnecessary confusion. Christy found a price tag on her charts quickly weeded out the sceptics.

"Or maybe the woman was just nervous." Lennie tossed the magazine aside and swung her legs to the floor, her size ten foot barely missing the glass of ice tea on the coffee table. "You gotta remember, Christy, this fortune-telling stuff is scary for some people. It just smacks of the devil."

"If they feel that way, they should save their money and stick with the phony horoscopes in the newspaper," Christy snapped.

"That's a lousy attitude for a psychic advisor—

especially one who needs cash as badly as you do."

Christy slipped off her glasses and rubbed her eyes. All too often people changed their minds after requesting a chart. While having someone cast a personal horoscope sounded like fun, the idea of learning truths about yourself or knowing the future could be frightening. Paying for a horoscope meant you believed that destiny was affected by unknown forces. Some people weren't ready to make that leap. But a change of heart cost Christy more than a few dollars and her time. There was emotional barter going on. Every horoscope took a small part of her soul.

Lennie leaned forward and touched Christy's arm, "People just want a little reassurance. We know there's a future out there for us and we hope it's controlled by something other than chance and dumb luck. So we run to you, or to a psychic, or a gypsy fortuneteller, and we hope one of you sees the answer in their crystal ball." She grinned over at Christy. "I'm lucky. I live with an astrologer who has all the answers. So when am I going to win the lottery?"

Lennie's sudden philosophical bent surprised Christy and gave her something to think about. But not now. She picked a few horoscope books off the shelf and headed toward the bedroom. "You'll get rich when somebody dies," she called over her shoulder, "and everybody in your family is healthy as a horse."

"Yeah," she heard Lennie call after her, "we're a healthy herd all right. Maybe I'll have to kill one of them."

୧୨୧୨

The Perez woman was the first client since the horoscope Christy had done for Wolfe. As Christy opened the ephemeris, a rough draft of a chart fluttered from between the pages. She recognized it as Lloyd Parr's and hesitated before picking it up off the floor.

Wolfe did his disappearing act as soon as he got what he wanted from her. Two weeks later and she still felt raw from the encounter. She shook off the memory of that night and commanded herself not to dwell on the past, recent or otherwise. She replaced Parr's chart between random pages and turned to Emilina's September birth date.

Pulling out a horoscope blank, Christy began charting. Her practiced eye immediately spotted trouble. The woman was a Scorpio, made even more formidable by an Aries moon. Jupiter fell on the cusp of the ninth and tenth houses—and squared the natal sun. In balance to the Scorpion elements were equal parts of the sign of Virgo.

An astrological image of Emilina Perez exploded like a migraine headache into Christy's sub-conscious. It roiled with violence and anger, jealousy and dark passions. Shrewd. Demanding. Christy closed her eyes against sudden nausea and focused on the hazy image of a woman within the swirl of planets. Vain. Grasping. Christy spread her fingers and covered the chart, trying to gain control. She sensed hardships, a struggle between good and evil. Hunger for money. Drugs. Love. An image of a knife blade cut into the vision. Sharp eyes. Sharp tongue. Backbone of steel.

Careful, sister. She is a stronger force than you can deal with.

Christy's hands flew off the paper and her eyes burst opened.

The sense of dread was strong. Parr's horoscope jutted out from between the pages and taunted her. Two bad charts in a single month. She folded Emilina's rough draft in half and quickly locked it away in the desk drawer.

CHAPTER 8

It was Lennie's bowling night. Christy found herself grateful for a few hours of solitude each week as Lennie drove into Kearny to pursue her new-found passion. Christy strongly suspected Lennie's love for the sport had more to do with picking up men than knocking down pins.

The bowling kick had started a few weeks ago, and now Christy looked forward to her evenings alone. Lennie was good company most of the time, even though the country music and constant chatter grated on Christy's nerves. But, without Lennie, Christy knew she'd withdraw even deeper into her shell. She needed an extroverted roommate to push her back to the company of other people.

Still, Tuesday nights were hers. First *Jeopardy*, then she'd fill the claw-footed bathtub up to her chin with warm water and aroma therapy bath salts. A bath pillow for her head and a paperback was all she needed to enjoy a long soak. No Lennie pounding on the door wanting to know if she was a prune yet or hollering to use the toilet.

The phone rang and she automatically glanced over at the clock. The evening news was over, prime time re-runs wouldn't start for another hour. She picked up the phone. "Hi, Mom."

"I just can't surprise you, can I?"

Her mother sounded in a chatty mood. Christy settled comfortably in the wide seat of the chair and swung her legs over the padded arm.

There was a routine to her mother's calls. She started with general inquiries into Christy's health—both physical and emotional—then moved quickly through polite questions about work. Her mother had never been employed outside the home and made it clear she disapproved of Christy's career choice.

Eventually, Mom would get to the reason for the call. But first Christy heard about the neighbors and the health of close family friends, small town gossip, and her mother's version of world events. And news of her globe-trotting dad.

"Your father is racking up the frequent flyer miles on these aeronautical consulting trips of his. He just doesn't know the meaning of retirement." Christy played with the TV remote as she listened, interjecting an appropriate

"Uh-huh" into the monologue when her mother paused for breath.

"I spoke to your sister the other day." Christy snapped off the TV and sat up. Calls from the convent were doled out sparingly throughout the year, usually around Holy Days. A call in mid-July meant something unusual was up.

"Celeste got promoted to Mother Superior and is being sent to a small convent in Illinois."

"That's quite an accomplishment at her age," Christy responded sincerely, but once again felt like the designated underachiever in the family.

Even among her Dominican sisters, Celeste stood out. When she donned the white habit and black veil, her inherited psychic abilities became a commodity of the Church. "Spiritual sensitivity" the nuns called it. Now they were promoting her. At this rate, she'd achieve sainthood in record time.

Once Celeste confided in her, instead of God, when they were children and the world was a place of many moves and strange homes as her father's career skyrocketed with the booming space industry. As a civilian attached to the air force, Roger Bristol kept on the move from base to base, and his family followed like nomads. When they started school, Christy and Celeste realized they didn't fit in—not with the air force brats and never with the children from town.

Celeste found continuity in the Catholic church. She knelt for hours in the cool recesses of St. Anthony's or St. Michael's or Blessed Trinity, a solemn child who drew the attention of priests and nuns. And she whispered to her younger sister secrets from the "voices." When she was eleven the voices told her she would give her life to God, and she stopped confiding in Christy altogether.

What Celeste found in the Church, Christy found in the library. She had library cards from a dozen towns, and she kept everyone, in case they ever moved back. School was torture—she missed multiplication completely when they moved three times during the third grade. The only education that mattered was found between the covers of the books she toted home, and that knowledge was a closely guarded secret like the psychic games she played with Celeste.

Her father had no idea how his career affected his daughters, and her mother saw nothing wrong with her children spending their childhoods in churches and libraries. Later, when Celeste announced her plans to take vows, and Christy refused to take the SATs, they wondered exactly where they had failed as parents.

But the family adapted, as they had always done when confronted with change. Celeste became Sister Catherine, and Christy found her niche in law enforcement.

She tuned her mother back in. "I was wondering if

you could do a quick horoscope on your sister," she was saying.

"I don't think so, Mom."

"Why not?"

"I don't know—it just doesn't seem right to mix astrology and the Church. I don't want to push my luck."

"Don't be silly. Who's going to find out? I would never tell your sister. We'll keep it our little secret."

Christy shared plenty of "secrets" with her mother, and she suspected her mother had a few with Celeste and Grandma Good as well. But in a family fraught with psychics, secrets didn't remain secret for long.

"So are you seeing anyone special these days?"

"Just Lennie."

"Don't get smart with me. I mean, have you been dating?"

"Since you called last week? No."

"With all those handsome deputies you work with, surely there must be one you could go out with. They make good money and anyone can see they're family men. Even a divorced one would be fine."

As Christy passed the thirty-year mark, her mother became less stringent in her checklist. "Handsome" now included men with receding hairlines and less-than-perfect profiles. Divorced was acceptable and younger men a consideration. Race and religion were no longer issues. In fact, any available man with a job would do as a son-in-law.

"I saw James Wolfe two weeks ago, but it wasn't a date."

"Is he getting divorced?"

"No, Mom. We had dinner together at the Shanghai."

"You aren't trying, Christy. A pretty girl like you, in a job surrounded by men, you should be out dancing every night of the week. Before I met your father…"

Christy listened to the lines she knew by heart, the fairy tale she'd been told as soon as she became old enough to worry about boys. Regina Good, the Irish beauty from Quonset, Rhode Island, with porcelain skin and periwinkle eyes. Engaged five times, she kept all her engagement rings. Then along came a handsome Southerner, who swept her off her dancing feet and out to California where they lived happily ever after.

"You can't hide away in your room all the time, Christy," her mother continued. "You'll never meet a man that way. And remember, men don't like serious women. Put those books down, slip on a pretty dress, and go out. That's what I would do if I were your age."

The buzz of the doorbell made her jump. "Mom, someone's at the door."

"A date?"

"No, Mom. I've got to go. Call you later."

CHAPTER 9

She wasn't expecting company but she was glad she hadn't changed into her frayed night gown. Maybe it was Wolfe dropping by to apologize. The shorts and T-shirt she wore was presentable enough to at least open the door. Christy shot a glance at the hall mirror and smoothed her hair. At the door she called out, "Who is it?"

"Emilina Perez. You did my horoscope two weeks ago. I have some questions."

Scorpion woman. Of course, she had questions. Christy tried to be as diplomatic as possible without telling outright lies when she wrote Emilina's chart. She didn't believe in shielding customers from hard truths, but she knew how to take the sting out of the words.

Christy opened the door as wide as the chain lock would allow and peered out. Emilina had the primped-out look of a woman with too much time and cosmetics on her hands. Her breasts strained to filled a snug camisole top to the point of overflowing. She held her astrological chart with the tips of long, fuchsia fingernails.

"It's a little late, Ms. Perez. You should have called first. Usually, I meet clients at a public place, like a restaurant or the park—" Christy glanced at the woman's attire. "—or maybe a bar. I don't do business at my home."

"I lost your phone number, but I had your address." The woman leveled her dark, penetrating eyes. "I drove all the way from Faller to talk to you. I don't understand some of this shit in my chart. I paid you, so you gotta explain it to me."

Christy stared through the gap in the doorway with only a chain separating her from the woman's intimidations. But as she watched, the lids came half-way down on Emilina's eyes and a lazy smile softened her features. The woman shrugged. "Look, if you can't talk right now, okay, I understand. But it was a long drive over here, and I really gotta pee—at least let me use the toilet before I leave."

Christy felt guilty for being so cautious. Suspicion was a side effect of working at the sheriff's department, but she understood a full bladder. Muttering "Just a second," she closed the door and unchained it.

The door burst open. Heavy hands grabbed her by

the T-shirt. Two men wearing sunglasses and baseball caps pulled low over their foreheads slammed her up against the wall. Emilina stood to one side.

"Do everything I say or you'll get hurt. Do you understand?" said the one with the black, bushy beard.

Christy nodded.

"Anybody else here?"

She shook her head.

"You're coming with us. Keep it quiet and don't try anything stupid. Understand?"

When she didn't respond, the second man shoved a metal-cold object into her ribcage. She nodded vigorously.

"Get her purse," the first man commanded Emilina.

Over their heads came a knocking sound. Jonathan Maciel thumped his broom handle on the floor to let her know she was being too noisy. *Yes, Mr. Maciel, make a racket*, Christy prayed. *Come downstairs and yell at us.* The men looked at the ceiling then at each other.

"Let's get her out of here before someone comes," the bearded man told his partner.

He led the way down the narrow stairwell followed closely by Christy, the gunman, and Emilina. Christy let her feet fall heavily on the old boards and managed a slight stumble at the landing. She heard the creak of Maciel's door and looked up to see if he was watching the procession, but the gunman blocked her and pushed the weapon solidly into her ribs.

"Your neighbors better not butt in." His breath stank and his teeth were yellow.

A powder blue Cadillac that had seen better days waited in the driveway. Emilina moved ahead and opened the backseat door.

"Christy! Going out with friends tonight?" Mrs. Alcorn ambled up the walkway, a burlap sack filled with fruits and vegetables on her arm. She peered cheerfully, if myopically, at the foursome. Christy's abductors froze.

"Yes, I am, Mrs. Alcorn. Could you give my roommate a message?" The gun pressed a warning into her back. "Tell her the cat's missing, and she needs to look for it."

"Oh, I wouldn't worry, dear. Pets always manage to find their way home. I bought cream today, a little treat for my decaf—I'll put some out for your kitty." Mrs. Alcorn smiled serenely and waved goodbye as Christy was shoved into the backseat of the Caddy. Emilina sat at the far end, and Yellow Teeth got in next to Christy. She caught a glimpse of Maciel's beret-covered head craning out of the top story window. She hoped he got a good look.

The car took off, spewing gravel in its wake.

With her body pumping adrenalin, Christy tried to wrestle some control over her panic. Staring at a gun barrel less than two feet away made it difficult. She was used to seeing holstered guns on the hips of the deputies, but not the steel of a semi-automatic trained on her. She couldn't pull her eyes away.

Heat trapped inside the Cadillac turned the car into a sweatbox. There was no air conditioning and all the windows were rolled up. Christy felt sweat drip off her hairline and down her neck, making rivulets between her breasts. Her glasses slid down her nose and fogged. Emilina's black hair formed ringlets around her beaded forehead. The rank body odor of the two men smelled like onions. Christy hated the smell of onions. The first wave of nausea swept over her when the driver lit a cigarette.

Christy shut her eyes and breathed through her mouth. She was back on the bus in the fifth grade, a field trip to the dairy. Too many bodies packed into the bus, too many bumps, too much heat, and on top of that, the smell of manure. She threw up and ruined the trip for everyone. The kids never let her forget it. She was glad when her father moved them away from that town.

"Hey, are you okay?" She felt a hand roughly shaking her shoulder.

"I'm getting car sick. I need some air." On either side, bodies moved to give her room.

"She looks awful bad, Trimmer. Maybe we could crack the windows a little bit."

Emilina fanned her face with a flapping hand. "I'm getting hot back here too."

"Don't roll down the windows until we're out of

town," ordered the driver. "It might be a trick."

Christy felt the cool barrel of the revolver at her temple. The gunman leaned in and she held her breath to guard against his. "Lady, you puke in this car, and I'll make you pay."

No one spoke another word. Christy kept her eyes closed and her breathing controlled, focusing on the bile lodged in her throat. Her head swirled in confusion from the motion of the car, compounded by a fear so primal that it became another sickness for her body to deal with.

She had no idea how many minutes or how many miles had passed before she felt a rush of air. The odor of fermenting grapes told her they were in open country. She opened her eyes, blinking against the light, and strained hungrily toward the breeze inhaling large gulps of dry air. Looking out the window, Christy saw the green blur of grapevines growing so close to the roadway that their tendrils whipped at the car as it raced by. She leaned back on the seat and stared ahead as the Cadillac sped down the green corridor.

Her head cleared but the sickening realization that somehow, for some reason, she was a hostage continued to make her nauseous. Carefully, she took stock of her captors. The man next to her held the revolver loosely in his hand, the weight of the barrel cocking his thin wrist back like a mousetrap ready to snap. He appeared to be in his late twenties, very thin, with a blond moustache sparsely coating his upper lip, so light it looked like milk. The driver, "Trimmer," seemed a few years older and looked as though he worked out with weights. A black heart tattoo decorated his forearm.

A thousand questions screamed in Christy's mind, but she kept her lips pressed firmly together. Nobody in the car would give her any answers. Instead, she tried to make out street signs in the fading light so she would be able to report her location accurately to Dispatch when she was released. That thought comforted her for a brief millisecond before the cold truth hit—they were letting her watch their route because she wouldn't be alive to tell anyone. The wall of oleanders on the left-hand side of the road made Christy's breath catch sharply. The car slowed and turned into a gravel driveway. The mailbox, metal lip ajar and a pile of newspapers at the base, was all too familiar.

"Welcome to the compound," the driver said as the Cadillac swung sharply into a semi-circular driveway. Three massive dogs raced to the car in a frenzy of barking, flinging dog spit in all directions as they snapped at the door handles. "And here's the welcoming committee."

Christy thought he was referring to the animals until she looked at the house. There, in the doorway, a silhouette stood, waiting for his guest.

CHAPTER 10

His eyes weren't green, as listed in the computer files, but more of a steel gray. The dilated pupils gave them a hard, flat appearance, and the goatee made him look satanic. Faint lines of the shark tattoo jutted from the neck of a Harley Davidson tank top. He leaned against the doorframe as she was hustled inside.

The house had the sour smell of old cooking oil and unwashed laundry, the sweeter stench of rotting garbage, and the mustiness of surrounding fields. Once in the living room, her escorts released her and flopped on two mismatched and badly stained couches. Emilina positioned herself on the arm of one couch, stretched out across the back, and began massaging the shoulders of the one called Trimmer. Their host entered and made himself comfortable on the single piece of furniture that wasn't worn or torn. Only cigarette burns marred the Naugahyde of the easy chair.

Christy stood in the middle of the room, facing him. Frightened and wary, she cradled her arms against her chest and cupped an elbow tight in each hand to control her shaking.

"Do you know who I am?"

She met Lloyd Parr's eyes. "No."

"Why did you do my horoscope?"

Christy continued to stare but didn't answer. Better to wait and see where he was going with his questions. Parr took a manila envelope off the lamp stand and pulled out several typed pages.

"I know you did it." He tossed the pages at her. They separated and floated in the air. "I went to every astrologer in the area to do Emilina's chart. Yours was a match."

Uncrossing her arms, she picked up the pages scattered at her feet and pretended to study a few paragraphs. The papers rustled as her hands shook. The sun/moon logo in the left-hand corner was the giveaway.

"Yes, this is one of my horoscopes."

"Who told you to do it?"

She felt like a field mouse, staring into the cold gaze of a rattler. "I don't know."

"I've got a loaded Smith and Wesson here that says you do." He pulled the gun from his waistband and flicked off the safety.

Another gun barrel. She tried not to stare. "I got a phone call. A man just gave me a birth date and an address. Then he sent a money order, and I mailed him the horoscope. I never asked who it was for." The lie came out smoothly.

Parr put the safety back on and slipped the weapon back in his pants. He pulled at his beard and mulled over her answer. Trimmer, clearly bored with the interrogation, took a black lacquer box off the coffee table. Parr glared at him. He quickly put it back.

"This man got a name? What address did you mail it to?"

Christy knew her answer had to be convincing. Her mind worked faster than the computer at the substation as she sifted through all the information she'd pulled up on Parr. The Asshole file sprang from her memory banks.

"Marlin—or maybe Molin. The mailing address was somewhere north, either Washington or Oregon. That's all I remember."

Her lie worked like a soup bone thrown to a pack of dogs. Everyone in the room became animated.

"She's talking about Trace!"

"Sounds like something Malin would pull."

"Probably tracked this girl down just to play a little joke."

"He got you good this time, Lloyd."

Christy listened as the group gnawed over the lie and

swallowed it. Parr nodded at the comments, the flatness in his eyes replaced by uneasy amusement. She'd put everybody in a good mood. Maybe they would take her home.

The front door slammed. The banter stopped and heads turned to look past Christy. Cautiously, she glanced behind her. A heavy-set, gray-bearded man filled the doorway and stared at her through slitted eyes. Next to him stood a teenager wearing tattered Levis and a family resemblance.

"Is this the horoscope lady?" His voice was low and deep, like the growl of a grizzly.

"Yeah. She says Trace Malin put her up to it, Blood."

Joseph Youngblood Sr. looked Christy over. She felt the danger level in the room go up a notch.

"That's real interesting, Lloyd, 'cause the last word I got, that shithead was doing time in the Oregon State Pen. Maybe she knows something I don't."

The amusement died in Parr's eyes, leaving them darker and colder than ever. He looked at his lab man. "What do you think we should do?"

"I'll get ahold of a buddy upstate and find out if Malin's playing games from his prison cell. If he's out, I'll call the dickweed myself and find out where he got your birth date and why he pulled this stunt. Let's see if her story checks out. In the meantime—" Youngblood gave

Christy the once over. "—you nabbed yourself a live as-trologer, Lloyd. Maybe you should get this bullshit out of your system once and for all." He turned on his heel and walked out. The teenager followed.

Parr glared at Youngblood's back then at the two men on the couch. "Get out," he ordered. "One of you take Emilina home."

Once the two of them were alone, Parr ignored her. He picked up a black lacquer box off the table and took out a small baggie. Opening it, he slipped his thumb and forefinger in. With a pinch of powder halfway to his nose, he stopped and remembered his duties as host. "Want some?"

She shook her head.

He shrugged. "It's going to be a hellava long night. You might change your mind before it's over."

CHAPTER 11

Night dragged into early morning. Christy shifted on the cracked footstool and peeked at her watch. Two a.m. and Parr showed no signs of winding down. At regular intervals, he stopped, dipped into the lacquer box, and took a hit. From all the drug reports she'd processed at work, Christy realized he was taking hits of methamphetamine. Parr seemed in control, his body melded into the contours of the lounger, but his eyes were in constant motion, and his fingers drummed incessantly on the arm of the chair.

"I've always, ya know, been psychic. Like I've got ESP or something." He rattled the horoscope papers. "You saw it here in my chart. None of the other astrologers I talked to mentioned it. That's how I knew you were different."

She kept quiet, wondering where this latest trail of

conversation would lead. Early in the evening, when the others were sent from the room, Christy feared Parr would rape her. But sex appeared to be the furthest thing from the man's mind. She never got the impression that he looked at her as a woman, or that he saw her at all. His eyes wandered as he talked, looking her over from time to time, but never focusing on physical features. She'd always heard drugs killed the sex drive. Hopefully, it was true.

Once fear was set aside, Parr just became boring. Christy listened to his views on everything, from his scorn of society in general to his taste in music. He believed drugs should be legalized so he could sell openly, electricity should be free, and Mexican food gave him heartburn. He treated her like a willing audience, but this was no social visit. She kept her replies down to single syllables. Wrapped up in his own world, Parr never asked personal questions, and Christy didn't volunteer information. In between his rantings were long silences, stretches when he seemed lost in some internal dialogue while she fought off fatigue.

Now he wanted to talk about the horoscope that linked their lives. "The others think I'm crazy to believe in the occult," he said in low, confidential tones as his eyes swept the room. "But I know there are messages for me from the stars. There's this strange force guiding me. I just have trouble tuning into it sometimes."

What she wanted to say was "Did you ever think it might be the drugs scrambling your brain?" Instead, she volunteered, "Pisceans have strong intuition. They rule the twelfth house."

He looked confused.

"You know about the houses, don't you?"

He waved his hand impatiently, as though swatting aside the notion that the reference went over his head.

"Then you know the twelfth house governs the occult and intuition. It's the nature of your ruling sign."

"Is that why I see ghosts?"

Whoa. Maybe his haunted look wasn't just from addiction. "I noticed a higher than normal degree of ESP when I cast your chart, but I don't know how far it's developed." She looked at him with what she hoped was perceived as concern. "Do you really see ghosts?"

Parr bolted from the chair and paced the room. The agitation seemed to come from something other than the drugs he'd ingested. As she watched, Christy remembered she was here because Wolfe believed Parr murdered a snitch. And she knew other unsolved murders on the books were linked to Lloyd Parr—no solid proof but plenty of suspicion. Maybe he did see ghosts. Or maybe he was haunted by a guilty conscience.

He folded the papers in his hand and put them on the lamp stand. "I don't want to talk about the past. What I need from you is my future. Can you do that?"

"Yes, but my books are back in my apartment."

"I'll send one of my men to pick them up."

He reached down and grabbed the strap of her purse. She froze. Sergeant Traynor always chided her for leaving her ID badge at home, but now Christy prayed for bad habits. She definitely didn't want Parr to know she worked for the sheriff.

He unzipped the side compartment and pulled out her key ring. A slip of paper fell to the rug. "Show me your house key."

"I have a roommate. Please don't hurt her."

"What time does she leave for work?"

"Seven forty-five. The books are on a bookshelf, just as you enter the apartment. Middle shelf. There are seven books, but I only need—"

"We'll take all of them." Parr stood up, the night concluded. "You want a drink? Soda? Beer?"

It was the first time he'd offered something other than drugs. Fear left her mouth dry and her throat raw. Hunger pangs set in after the adrenalin subsided, but she knew that cranksters ignored food for long periods of time.

When Parr turned to set her purse on the coffee table, Christy reached down, snatched the piece of paper off the rug, and slipped it into the pocket of her shorts. Then she followed her host into the kitchen.

Roaches scattered when the light came on. A sink

spilled over with food-encrusted dishes. Garbage overflowed the trash can. Christy averted her eyes when he
opened the refrigerator, afraid to look. He handed her a
sticky can of grape soda then walked her down the hall
and stopped at the second door. On the floor was a filthy
mattress with an equally dirty sheet on top of it. A barred
window framed by green curtains prevented escape. The
room came with a private bathroom, but no light bulbs.

"Don't open the window, it's alarmed. The dogs are
loose at night, and I've got guards. Don't get any smart
ideas about leaving." He shut the door, turned the bolt
lock, and left.

Christy stood in complete darkness except for a sliver of moonlight coming through the bars. She found the
bathroom, washed the soda can before popping it open,
and willed herself to sip, not gulp. It felt good to be left
alone with her fear, to give in to it away from Parr's scrutiny. False bravado drained her. The next few hours were
going to require all her stamina. She needed to sleep. But
not on the mattress. Something about it sent chills
through her. Christy backed to the far corner of the room
and curled up on the carpet.

I'm here with you, sister.

"I know, Celeste. I know."

The sun illuminates
and intensifies.

CHAPTER 12

Lennie roused herself from an uneasy night of half-sleep and hurried to check her roommate's bed. It was still in pristine order in the infuriatingly tidy manner that Christy always kept it, side seams lined up on the bedspread and throw pillows precisely thrown. Her roommate had clearly slept somewhere else last night.

Lennie grabbed the first pair of clean pants she found in her closet and a top that needed ironing, but only if you looked carefully. She tucked it in to smooth the wrinkles, pared her twenty minute makeup routine down to two, and raced out the door.

She made the ten minute trip to the substation in record time. Sergeant Traynor was halfway across the parking lot when she pulled up. Seeing Lennie arrive fifteen minutes early for work made him stop dead in his tracks.

"Aren't you the early bird? Where's your roommate? Is her Fiat finally fixed?"

"No, Sarge. I'm kinda hoping Christy's inside because she sure didn't spend the night in her own bed."

Lennie immediately cursed her loose tongue. She saw Traynor cock an eyebrow but he curtailed his curiosity. She knew Christy was his golden girl, although he tried not to play favorites. The last thing Lennie wanted to insinuate was that her roommate slept around. At least, not on week nights.

Christy wasn't inside the substation but, as Traynor said, it was still early. Maybe she went to pick up her car, or maybe she'd overslept, wherever she was sleeping. At any rate, Christy was reliable and knew the rules. Traynor was sure she would call in.

When no call came by ten o'clock, Traynor asked one of the deputies to man the phones and told Lennie to pour herself a cup of coffee and come into his office.

"Tell me everything you can think of, starting with the last time you saw Christy." Traynor pushed a donut box toward her.

As upset as she felt about her missing roommate, it didn't stop Lennie's stomach from growling. She reached for a bear claw.

"The last time I saw her was at home. That was about six-thirty last night."

"What was she wearing?"

Lennie thought a minute. "Blue shorts and a white T-shirt. I told her I was heading out to Kearny for my bowling night, and she said she'd be home, watching TV."

"So you went bowling and she seemed okay when you left?"

She shifted in the chair. "Well, no and yes. I didn't really go bowling, that was a lie. But yeah, she was fine when I left."

"Why did you lie to her?"

Lennie popped the last bite of pastry into her mouth. She chewed slowly and wiped the corners then took a long sip of coffee to wash it down. There was no way to stall his question. "Every Tuesday I tell her I'm bowling, but I've been sneaking to out to typing classes at the adult school. I wanted to surprise you and Christy. I'm up to thirty-five words a minute."

A smile shadowed Traynor's features before he became all business again. "So you had a secret that you kept from your roommate. Is it possible she's got a secret she keeps from you?"

"Christy? No, sir, I can read her like yesterday's mail."

"What if she was having an affair with a married man? Do you think she'd tell you something like that?"

"Come on, Sarge. We're talking about Christy here. Anyway, she wouldn't have to tell me because she'd act so guilty, I'd figure it out."

"Sometimes you think you know people, even people you live with for years, and yet they'll pull some real surprises on you." Traynor's divorce was only three months old, and he was still in a baffled state. "Christy's a grown woman, and we can't presume to know her business. All we know for sure is that she's spent one night away from home and hasn't shown up for work or called in."

They looked at each other across the desk for a long minute, then both reached into the donut box.

"What about her folks? Don't they live in the next county? Maybe she had a family emergency."

"I thought about that, but I don't want to scare her family by calling and asking if they've seen her. Besides, we have a chalkboard by the refrigerator where we leave messages. And she would have called in by now, unless she's in some kind of trouble." Having finally expressed her worst suspicions, Lennie put down the jelly donut. She'd lost her appetite.

"We can't write up a missing persons report for at least forty-eight hours. Those are the rules, Lennie."

"That's what you tell civilians, but we can bend the rules for Christy, can't we, Sarge? She's one of us, and she could be in real danger."

"We don't know that for sure." Worry lines furrowed his forehead. "I'll mention to patrol units at Watch III briefing to keep an eye out for her. And I'll call the repair shop to see if she's paid the ransom on her Fiat within the last twenty-four hours. If it's on the road, I'll pass the plate number and description to the men. We don't need to involve dispatch or issue a BOL over the teletype yet. We'll keep it low-key and unofficial."

He stood up and crumbs tumbled off his uniform. "Why don't you go home for an early lunch and see if she's been by the apartment. Check her closet, see if any clothes are missing, if her luggage is still there. And see if she took her toothbrush."

Lennie nodded her head. She couldn't concentrate on work with all this on her mind, no sense wasting the county's money.

❧❦❧

When Lennie arrived at the apartment, Mrs. Alcorn stood on the front steps, giving them a good sweep. She paused to let Lennie pass.

"Have you found your kitty yet?"

"Excuse me?"

"Your kitty. I've put cream out, but I haven't seen a sign of her. Your roommate said to tell you the kitty is missing, but you got in so late last night and left early this morning that I couldn't catch you."

The kitty's missing? Lord, the landlady's deck was short a few aces. Lennie thanked her politely for the message and headed up the stairs.

When she opened the door of the apartment, she saw dozens of books on the floor, thrown willy-nilly and lying open with pages bent.

"Christy?" Lennie called out tentatively. "Christy!" she repeated urgently.

She ran down the hall. Nothing appeared touched in Christy's room. She peeked in the bathroom and saw her roommate's turquoise toothbrush still in the holder. Glancing into her own room, she noticed lingerie spilling out of her drawer. She didn't remember making that much of a mess when she dressed this morning.

The phone startled her when it rang. She raced to the kitchen and grabbed a potholder before touching the receiver, mindful of fingerprints.

"Is she there?"

"No, Sarge, but somebody's been here. Books are dumped all over the floor. And I think somebody's been in my underwear."

"Don't touch anything, Lennie. I'm on my way with a fingerprint kit."

"Wait. There's something else. Christy told the landlady that our cat is missing." Lennie took a ragged breath. "Sergeant, we don't own a cat."

CHAPTER 13

Christy tensed when she saw the astrology books in Neeley's spindly arms. He held all seven books at once, leering his piss-colored grin at her. She hated him at that moment, hated the way his nicotine-stained fingers curled around the spines of the books, imprinting the bindings with filth. She felt physically violated.

"Mission accomplished." He opened his arms and the books fell to the floor.

Christy dropped to her knees and picked them up. As she cradled the books tightly in her arms, she felt a wave of homesickness pass through her. The worn pages smelled of apartment greenery and warm cups of tea by the fire. Something of herself was embedded in the books. Her thumbs had dog-eared the corners, and in the margins were notes, faded but memorized over the years.

My books, she recited like a prayer as she clutched the books to her chest. *Mine*.

Parr stood behind Neeley.

"Everything go okay?"

"Yeah, no problem. The old lady was there, but I don't think she saw me."

Parr grunted then looked down at Christy. "You've got your books, get started on my future."

Christy stood up and surveyed the room.

"I need a desk or table to write on. And a chair. And a light bulb, unless you want me to quit working when it gets dark. I could use some light in the bathroom too."

Par looked at Neeley. "Get her what she wants."

"Why can't she work on the kitchen table?"

"I need privacy. It takes concentration," she interjected.

Neeley started to whine, but Parr cut him short. "Just get it."

"I could also use pens and some blank paper." Parr looked at her as though she were asking for raspberries in December. "Or lined. Whatever you have in the house."

"Lady, we don't have any of that stuff."

Parr stomped out of the room, followed by Neeley. She heard the lock secured with a sharp click.

Alone again. She'd already spent eight hours of solitary huddled in the far corner of the room, keeping one eye on the door between winks of sleep. All night thoughts raced through her mind, running the gamut from sheer terror of Parr to pure hatred of Wolfe. Damn Wolfe. It was all his fault.

Or, maybe not.

The books were biting into her arms. The window sill looked wide enough to hold them. Christy blew off the dust and set the books down. She brushed away a spider's web, pushed back the sheer green curtains, and arranged the volumes by height, in the order they sat on her shelves at home. She nudged one book into alignment with the rest. An angry tear spilled and soaked into the pages.

I had to show Wolfe, she chided herself. *Stupid, stupid pride. I had to prove my astrology worked. Look where it got me.*

The room felt suffocatingly close. She reached up for the catch on the window, dying to slide the glass over and breathe in fresh air. Maybe the alarm system was all a bluff. Her hand reluctantly moved away. Maybe not. She wasn't sure how far she could push her abductors or her luck, and she didn't feel particularly brave. Through the grimy pane, she looked out over acres of vines lined up in regimental rows. Rays of sun sliced through the dusty haze. For a second, Christy worried the intense sun would bleach the book covers if they sat in the window. But that would take time. Whatever happened, her stay would be short.

CHAPTER 14

Christy heard movement in the hall and the click of the lock. The door swung open wide enough to admit Emilina then closed and locked behind her.

Hanging off the woman's shoulder was an oversized canvas bag emblazoned with a colorful montage of palm trees and beach umbrellas and the words "Fun in the Sun" embroidered across the front. "Lloyd told me to bring you some stuff."

She dropped the bag to the floor with a shrug of her shoulder and pushed it toward Christy with the toe of a worn pump. Basic black appeared to be Emilina's fashion statement, despite the summer heat. Today she wore a black tank top which failed to cover graying bra straps, skin-tight jeans with ankle zippers, and patent leather pumps. She looked dark and dangerous.

Christy had a feeling it was intentional.

Keeping an eye on the woman, Christy stooped and picked up the bag. She extracted a pink bath towel, worn from many washings and stiff from drying on a clothesline. When she brought it close to her face, it smelled like fresh air.

"I brought soap too. They don't wash their hands around here, so I know they don't got any."

Christy reached in and found the bar of soap. It was wrapped in purple tissue paper and sealed with a label decorated with lilacs

"Nice."

"Yeah. Just something I found in a drawer from last Christmas."

"Thanks. I appreciate this. I need to wash up."

There was one more item in the bag—a roll of toilet paper. Christy closed her eyes and gave a silent prayer of thanks.

The woman turned and rapped on the door then cocked her head and listened. "They forgot about me." Swearing under her breath, she flopped on the mattress and kicked her heels off. Christy put the toiletries in the bathroom and resumed her place on the floor across from Emilinia.

"This used to be our room," Emilina said, looking around. "I put those curtains up."

"Were you and Parr...

"Hard to believe, huh? That was a long time ago, almost eight years. He was different then. Not much different 'cause he was always a sonofabitch, and he hurt anybody who got in his way. But the house was okay, and I kept it clean."

Christy tried to picture a much younger Emilina, late twenties, with an apron tied around her waist and a dust cloth in her hand. The track marks marring the inside of Emilina's arms belied the image.

"We did a cook every couple of weeks, and we had about ten runners selling for us. I had plenty of nice clothes, and I gave money to my family. We were living good."

Christy found herself repelled and fascinated by details of the drug culture. "What happened?"

"Lloyd liked the powder too much. We was making plenty of the stuff. He kept big bowls of crank in every room, like candy dishes—nose candy." She let loose with a harsh laugh. "He was always crazy, and he got worse the more crank he shoved up his nose and his veins. Then he wasn't a man no more, he was…"

"Impotent?"

"Yeah. He couldn't get it up. It was over between us."

It was a relief to hear Emilina confirm the substation stories about drugs and diminishing sexual drive. Still, Christy had to be sure.

"Emilina, am I in any physical danger here?"

The woman narrowed her eyes and curled her lips in a sneer, wiping out the last remnants of beauty left in her face. "You worried about being gang raped? I thought you could see into the future."

"I looked. There's nothing there."

It was a lie, but it stopped Emilina short.

"There's nothing there because these guys don't want you that way. Neeley don't want pussy period—he only wants crank. Joey's too young to know what he wants. And Trimmer's my man now, so he better not touch you."

Emilina pushed herself off the mattress and picked up the empty satchel. Perspiration shined her skin and several coats of mascara swam in the bags of her eyes. She stretched like a cat.

"Anyway, you're Lloyd's fortune teller now. He'll kill anybody who touches you. And don't worry about him. You're not his type."

The question of rape had worried Christy more than once since her abduction. Now she felt she could set that fear aside.

"Why do you come back if it's over between you and Lloyd?" Christy asked. "I wrote in your chart that you had a real problem with men in your life, that you always pick men who are bad for you and will hurt you. They used you to grab me yesterday. They couldn't have done it without you. Why do you let these men manipulate you like that? It's not for sex, it's not for money—so what is it? You can do better, you know."

"Yeah, right. That was some chart you did. When I read it, I knew you were for real because none of the other astrologers chewed my butt. So what, if I helped them kidnap you? I wanted to meet you after I read all that stuff you wrote about me. But don't worry about me. I'm gonna find a dealer with some real cash to take care of me."

She gave three sharp raps on the door, and they heard footsteps coming down the hallway. She turned and looked at Christy. "If you want to worry about something, *chica*, worry about Blood. He hates this astrology shit, and he's pissed that you're here. They say his father was a quarter Apache, so he has just enough Indian blood in him to be dangerous. If he wants to hurt you, rape would be getting off easy."

CHAPTER 15

Sergeant Traynor stood in the middle of the living room, his hands blackened with print dust and two smudges on his face, one on the forehead and the other to the side of his nose. He was pleased with the search.

A good handprint surfaced on the refrigerator, and what appeared to be a thumbprint showed on the dust cover of a hardbound Michener. Both dressers were dotted with prints on the lingerie drawers.

Lennie stared at the ransacked bookshelf, puzzling over the mess on the floor, wondering if they owned any books worth stealing. She couldn't remember titles, but their library was mostly paperbacks, and used at that. Still, Lennie felt she should know if any books were missing.

Suddenly, she did.

"Oh lord, Sergeant. Christy's astrology books are gone."

"Are you sure?"

She nodded. "She had at least a half dozen. They're not here."

"Do you think one of her customers broke in and took them? There's a lot of weirdos who believe in that stuff."

"She wasn't doing too many charts. But a Mexican woman called last week." Some bit of information nagged at Lennie's memory. "And James Wolfe dropped by the office during the heat wave. When was that—the early part of July?" Traynor nodded. "He took Christy outside for a private talk. She told me later he wanted a horoscope, but she clammed up, and I couldn't get any more out of her." Lennie looked at her sergeant and weighed her words. "She worried she might be breaking some rules by helping him."

"Sounds like we'd better have a talk with Detective Wolfe. But stolen books and horoscopes still don't explain Christy's disappearance." He brushed print dust from his hands. "Let's go downstairs and get a statement from your landlady."

Mrs. Alcorn hovered at the bottom of the stairwell, curious about the uniformed deputy in her building but careful not to interfere.

"Afternoon, ma'am." Traynor introduced himself.

"Could you tell me the last time you saw your tenant, Christy Bristol?"

"You have smudges on your face. Come inside and wash up." She led the sergeant and Lennie into her apartment and disappeared down the hallway.

Lennie had peeked through the door once or twice, but had never been inside Mrs. Alcorn's home. The place was decorated in pink, the predominant shade being Pepto Bismol. Accenting the pink were lace and frills. If it was meant to be homey, it missed the mark, despite the dozens of needlepoint pillows strewn about. The sergeant stood uncomfortably in the living room and kept a tight rein on his hands, which were embedded with graphite. Lennie could feel her auburn hair clashing with the decor.

Mrs. Alcorn came out of the bathroom and handed Traynor a rose-colored washcloth. "Let me think. I saw Christy last evening as I walked home from Soto's Market. I like shopping there, they sell bruised fruit and wilted vegetables for half price. It's perfectly good food, you understand." She smiled at her visitors. "Is this about the lost kitten? Christy didn't tell me its name or what it looks like. You people at the sheriff's department certainly take lost pets seriously."

"Did Christy tell you where she was going, Mrs. Alcorn?" The sergeant dabbed at his face and wiped his hands before handing back the washcloth.

She folded the grimy washcloth and placed it on a

marble table. "Well, I think it must have been a double date. There were two men and a woman with her. They seemed in a big hurry."

"Could you describe the men?"

Mrs. Alcorn smiled sweetly at the sergeant. "My eyes aren't very good when it comes to details, Officer. But let me think. They weren't dressed very nicely— jeans, T-shirts, and baseball caps. One had bushy black hair, a dark beard and tattoos. The other was fair and had some hair on his chin. The woman with them looked very…" She searched for the proper adjective, "flashy."

"Were they Caucasian?"

She gave them a confused look. "I don't know. I suppose so. Is that important?"

Traynor tried a different approach. "What about a car? Did they drive up in a car?"

"Oh, they had a big car. Not a very nice one, but then cars are so expensive these days. It was robin's egg blue. They were in such a hurry to leave that they made a mess of the gravel." Mrs. Alcorn shook her head disapprovingly.

Footsteps sounded on the stairwell and Lennie glanced out in time to see Jonathan Maciel's backside disappear around the landing. She tapped Traynor's arm and cocked her head toward the door.

"All these questions. Is Christy in some kind of trouble?" The landlady followed her company to the door, reluctant to lose the sergeant's attention.

Lennie edged toward the stairs. "She hasn't come home yet. We're just wondering where she could be."

"First your kitten, now your roommate. No telling what will disappear next."

"You've been a big help, ma'am. We'll check on your leads." Traynor backed out of the apartment and into the neutral shades of the hallway.

Jonathan Maciel was reluctant to open the door more than a crack, even after Traynor identified himself and showed the man his badge. Finally, Maciel rolled his eyes heavenward and flung the door open.

"Come in, come in, let's get it over with. This is about the car license I called in last night, isn't it? I'm surprised the sheriff's department is so slow to respond, especially since it's one of your own people."

"What are you talking about?" Traynor bristled.

"The call I made regarding the abduction of my downstairs neighbor, this young woman's roommate. I called in the license just after eight o'clock last night." He hurled himself into the cushions of a paisley couch and picked up a delicate china teacup and saucer. He did not offer them a seat or a jasmine tea.

"Are you saying Christy was abducted?" Lennie asked in disbelief.

"It certainly looked that way from where I stood. First, I heard all this racket coming from your apartment—doors slamming, loud footsteps—so I finally had to step out in the hall to see what was going on. They were headed down the stairs, all pressed up against each other. I went back inside and looked out my dormer window just in time to watch them push your friend into the backseat of a gas guzzler. They took off so fast the car fishtailed leaving the driveway. It was all very dramatic." He crossed his arms and sealed his lips in a thin line.

"Can you describe the people she left with?" Traynor scribbled furiously on his notepad.

"A woman and two despicable-looking men. One was quite hairy, and they both wore grimy T-shirts, torn Levis, sneakers, and baseball caps." He touched his own beret protectively.

He even wears it indoors, Lennie mused.

"Caucasian?"

"Underneath the dirt, yes, I suppose they were. Except for the woman—she looked Hispanic. And overdressed, I might add. Your friend wore shorts and a T-shirt."

"Do you still have the license plate number?"

Maciel got up and went to the Queen Anne writing desk. He pulled a cream-colored note with scalloped edges off a notepad and thrust it at the sergeant.

"I believe you'll find this accurate. My eyes are very sharp."

"I'll bet they don't miss a trick," replied Traynor.

CHAPTER 16

Traynor radioed in the license plate to dispatch as soon as he and Lennie were buckled in the patrol car and heading northbound out of Coronita. Then he turned his attention to Lennie.

"What has Christy got herself mixed up in? These don't sound like the kind of people she would hang out with."

"Not that girl. But I tell you, it sounds like the type Wolfe would be investigating."

They both looked at each other. Wolfe was bad news. Time to check in.

Traynor picked up his cell phone and dialed the Area I narcotics unit. The secretary connected him to Sergeant Perrelli's cell phone.

"What is it, Traynor?" Perrelli's voice cackled with static. "We're on a surveillance."

"I'm heading to your office on an urgent matter. I need to talk to you and Detective Wolfe."

"What the hell is this about, Traynor? I've got a man under and I can't just call the operation off because you've got a wild hair up your—hey, guys, who's got point? Did anybody get the plate of that Chevy pickup pulling into the driveway?" Perrelli turned his attention back to Traynor. "Whatever your beef is, we can meet later or I'll work you in tomorrow. I don't have time to chat right now."

"Fine. I'll take my problem to Internal Affairs. Maybe you can make time for their investigation."

"Whoa, hold on, Traynor. Don't go jumping the gun." Traynor heard Perrelli go to his radio. "Adam Nineteen, take over for me. Adam Forty-Two, head back to the office, ASAP." He returned on the line to Traynor. "Okay, we're en route. Meet you at the trailer. This better be important."

Lennie settled into the wide seat of the patrol car and let the chill of the air conditioner wash over her. Questions were being answered, but the answers were ominous. She looked across at Traynor, her view partially blocked by the shotgun resting upright between them. What she could see of his face looked grim and determined.

"Two Ida Thirty." The dispatcher's voice cut sharply through Lennie's thoughts. Traynor grabbed the mike.

"Ida Thirty. Go ahead."

The dispatcher repeated the license plate number Traynor had requested a check on, and added, "That plate comes back stolen."

"Ida Thirty, copy." He replaced the mike and looked over at Lennie. "I'm not surprised. Well, there goes one lead. Let's hope the Cal-ID system kicks out a match on the fingerprints."

They passed the narcotics trailer and made a U-turn on the deserted road. The double-wide trailer sat well off the main highway under a grove of oak and eucalyptus, looking for all the world like one of the farm trailers that dotted the countryside. A large barn stood to the left of the trailer and was used to keep undercover cars out of view. The Kings River flowed past the site.

The secretary waited at the top of the stairs, enjoying a cigarette. She let Traynor and Lennie into the office, curious but trained not to ask questions. She pointed to the coffeemaker and water dispenser. "There's sodas in the fridge. Fifty cents."

Lennie fished out two quarters and bought herself a cream soda. She looked around the crowded trailer. Pictures decorated bulletin boards, trophy shots of detectives posing with kilos of cocaine or bushy marijuana plants. *The thrill of the hunt*, she thought.

The main room was crowded with desks and file cabinets shoved into every available square inch of space.

Hanging on the wall was a burlap bag with the words "Marijuana 50 kilos" and a picture of a burro on it. It looked authentic, but Lennie had seen the identical bag in a local import shop. The framed marijuana leaf above one of the desks was the real thing. She edged in for a closer look.

"We confiscated it from a drug dealer's photo album. It's a nice piece of memorabilia." The secretary of the unit came out of her office, which would be the master bedroom in a normal trailer. Her work space was larger than the sergeant's, letting everyone know who the real boss was in the office.

Sergeant Perrelli and Detective Wolfe entered the trailer and walked past them to the sergeant's office in the rear. Traynor and Lennie followed, and Perrelli closed the door.

"What the hell is this all about?" Perrelli sat behind a formica desk and sifted through his messages while he waited for a reply.

"I want to ask Detective Wolfe about the horoscope he had my office assistant do for him in early July."

Perrelli started to let loose with a string of cuss words until he saw the stunned look on the detective's face. "Care to fill us in, Wolfe?"

"It was a personal matter."

"Not anymore. It's a departmental matter, and I need to know what you and Christy were up to," Traynor said.

"I asked her to do a horoscope, that's all. No big deal. What did Christy say about it?" Wolfe tried to look defiant.

Before Traynor could stop her, Lennie grabbed his arm and twisted Wolfe around. "She didn't say anything because she's been missing since last night. Today, somebody got into the apartment and took all her astrology books. I know you two were up to something because she kept it a secret, and she usually tells me everything. So if you know what's going on—" She tightened her grip on his muscular forearm. "—you'd better spill it."

Wolfe shook his arm free and looked around the room. All eyes were on him.

"I had her do Lloyd Parr's horoscope," he mumbled.

The sergeants looked at each other. "Why would you do a fool thing like that?" Perrelli demanded.

Wolfe nervously ran both hands through his hair. "I found out the guy was heavy into astrology. I was trying to draw him out, see if he'd lead me to Johnny Blue."

Traynor looked at Perrelli in disgust. "Is this how narcotics detectives do investigations in your unit? Through witchcraft?"

"First I've heard of it." Perrelli leveled his gaze at Wolfe. "You used an office assistant from another unit on a confidential case. Okay. What did you do with this horoscope?"

"We delivered it to his house."

"Tell me you didn't drive your undercover car."

Wolfe stared glumly at his sergeant.

Perrelli slammed his fist on top of the desk. "What in the hell were you thinking of? First, you bait a suspect and risk blowing the case, then you go joy riding with a civilian in your UC vehicle. I'll have your badge for this."

"Using an undercover car is the least of your worries. I've got a woman missing."

"Parr couldn't have found out who did it. It can't be connected." Wolfe was sweating and there was doubt in his voice.

"Christy had another horoscope right after you asked for one," Lennie said. All eyes turned to her. "It was a woman by the name of Emilina Perez. Do you know anything about that."

"Shit!"

Perrelli stood up and glared at the detective. "What the hell have you done, Wolfe?"

"That's Parr's girlfriend."

Traynor had heard enough. "I'll put together a search warrant and call the watch commander for SWAT."

"No!" Perrelli and Wolfe said in unison.

Traynor grabbed for the phone. "If Christy's in that house, we've got to get her out."

Perrelli moved the phone out of Traynor's reach. "Mitch, you're about to ruin an operation that's taken over seven months to put together. Why don't you hold off, and let's talk about this for a second?"

"I don't think there's much to talk about. Your detective put one of my office assistants in a life-threatening situation. Now, if you don't think that's as important as some undercover operation you've got cooked up, then maybe I should take this higher—say, to your captain, or even Sheriff Nolan." He turned toward the door.

Perrelli shot out from behind his desk and intercepted Traynor. "Come on, we started out in patrol together. We can solve this problem without the brass. Look, we don't even know if she's really been kidnaped, or if she's even in Parr's compound. Let's just cool down and work on this together."

As he was speaking, Perrelli placed a firm hand on Lennie's shoulder, opened the office door, and propelled her out of the room. Wolfe followed. As the door closed, Lennie heard Perrelli say, "I've got an idea that might solve both our problems."

The secretary was straining to hear what was going on behind closed doors. Lennie motioned Wolfe to follow her outside.

She sat down on a bench next to a redwood picnic table. "Wolfe, I can't sit here and do nothing as long as Christy's in trouble."

"It's out of our hands, Lennie. Let the sergeants handle it."

She gave Wolfe a sideways glance. "You know their hands are tied with red tape. By the time they get everybody's permission to check the place out, it could be too late."

Wolfe glared at the closed door. "I got her into this mess. They ought to at least let me in on their plans."

"I'm telling you, they'll hash this around until it's too late to do any good. Tell me where this Parr fella lives, and I'll go get Christy out of there."

"Don't be stupid."

Without warning, Lennie stood up and belted Wolfe in the shoulder, toppling him off the edge of the picnic table where he was perched. He fell and hit a trashcan and sent it careening across the cement. The secretary peeked out the sliding glass door then shrugged and went back to her office.

"What the hell's going on out here?" Perrelli looked out at the detective sprawled on the patio. He looked at Lennie's reddened face. "I asked you to wait. I didn't tell you to beat up my detective."

Traynor stepped in. "Why don't you let Wolfe run Lennie back to Coronita while we finish our discussion?"

"Get out of here," Perrelli ordered Wolfe. "And don't let her whip your ass on the ride into town. Once you drop her off, you're secured for the day. I don't want to see you until I cool off."

"Yes, sir." Wolfe picked himself off the cement, his

pride wounded but pleased to be getting out of the office early.

Once settled in the crankmobile, Lennie muttered an apology for the sucker punch.

"You caught me with my guard down, but you really pack a lot of power in that fist of yours."

"I used to beat up my ex when he needed it." Lennie flexed the fingers on her right hand proudly. "I'd like to get my hands on those lowlifes holding Christy."

Wolfe stared at the empty stretch of highway ahead. "I've been thinking about what you said, and you're right. If we wait for the sergeants to go through official channels, anything could happen to Christy. They won't make a move until they have proof she's in the compound."

"How do we get proof?"

"I might have a way to slip in, but you can't be part of this." She started to protest, but Wolfe stopped her. "No, I'm serious, Lennie. I know you want to help, but you don't know what you're dealing with. And, like you pointed out, I got her into this jam. It's up to me to get her rescued."

"What's your plan?"

"It's better if you don't know. That way, if I screw up, Internal Affairs can't come after you. I'd hate to see you lose your job."

Lennie crossed her arms and slouched down into the

seat. "You're just plain bad luck to be around, you know that, Wolfe?"

As they rode the rest of the way in silence, Wolfe fine-tuned his plan, and Lennie worked out a back-up plan in case the detective let her down.

Jupiter produces a feeling of optimism.

CHAPTER 17

After twenty hours of inhaling the noxious stench of Parr's house, Christy felt sure her sense of smell was dead. Which is why she was surprised to find herself anxiously sniffing the air like a prized retriever. Two distinct odors caught her attention, one being the sweet, heavy scent of marijuana, which she remembered from high school assemblies. The other was food.

The door to her room opened and Trimmer poked his head inside. "Chow time," he said and jerked his head of dark, unruly curls in the direction of the kitchen. She followed him out and down the hallway.

Everyone, except Blood, sat around the kitchen table, which had been cleared off by the sweep of someone's arm. The debris was scattered on the floor. Joey carefully set paper plates on the grimy surface. Several large bags with the words "Chili Chuckwagon" emblazoned on the side and a twelve pack of beer served as a centerpiece. Parr pointed to the empty seat next to him and muttered, "Sit."

She didn't know who gave the signal, but suddenly hands dove into the bags, tossing out an assortment of chili dogs, chili fries, chili burgers, and Styrofoam bowls of chili. A foot-long hot dog smothered in chili and covered with onions found its way to her plate. Someone shoved a cold beer in her direction.

Even hunger couldn't make the food look appealing. Christy stole a glance over at Parr, who picked at a few French fries without enthusiasm. She turned back to her own plate and re-evaluated her dinner. It looked disgusting. The greasy chili had sogged through the bun, making the hot dog tricky to pick up. She tried holding both ends, but the bottom dissolved upon lift-off and the hot dog slid out of her grasp and off the plate.

"Something wrong with the food?" Parr's voice held a dangerous note.

"It's fine." She dropped the bun ends on the plate and looked for a napkin to wipe chili off her fingers.

"I'll eat it if she don't want it," Neeley volunteered. He reached for the paper plate, but Parr knocked his hand away without taking his eyes off Christy.

"Eat or starve," he warned.

"Yeah, what's another dead body around the house,

huh Lloyd?" Trimmer tipped his chair back and rocked slightly, pleased with his joke.

The room fell deathly quiet. Parr turned his gaze slowly in Trimmer's direction. Rage filled his eyes. Without warning, his foot shot out and kicked Trimmer's chair. The impact drove him into the edge of the sink and the back of his head split open. A smear of blood followed as he crumpled in a heap at the baseboard.

"Next time you bring that up, I'll kill you."

Christy pushed her plate away and stood up. She had to get out. Her foot stumbled over Trimmer as she headed toward the door.

"Hold it!" The command cut through the air and she stopped but did not turn around. She could hear the others breathing uneasily. "Where do you think you're going?"

"Back to my room." She weighed the silence at her back but refused to turn around.

"Our table manners bother you, lady?"

She turned to face him. His gun was drawn.

"That—and the food. I'm used to eating a little healthier."

"Then I guess you'll starve." He motioned Neeley to take her down the hallway.

She knew he meant it and knew she had to keep her strength up and be alert. "Without something to eat, I won't be able to think clearly enough to cast your future."

She watched Parr weigh his options.

"What do you eat?" he finally asked.

"A few pieces of fresh fruit would be good."

Neeley sniggered. "Fruit!"

"It's in season, it's cheap, and there's a fruit stand on every corner this time of year." She could hear the stubbornness in her voice.

Parr picked up on it too. "Okay, we'll get fruit. Is that it?"

"Milk."

Parr narrowed his eyes.

"Lowfat. Whole grain bread. Luncheon meat and a small jar of mayonnaise." She wound up her list in a rush before anyone could interrupt.

"Write it down," Parr ordered Joey. "Anything else?"

She heard the sarcasm in his voice, but plowed ahead anyway. "Salad." They all looked at her quizzically, even Trimmer, who pulled himself up by holding on to the counter.

"A head of lettuce, tomatoes, cucumber, maybe a few radishes." Joey struggled to keep up. "I guess fat free dressing would be pushing my luck," she added.

"Yeah, it would, and your luck's running out fast." Parr fished in his pockets for two twenty dollar bills.

It was a small victory, but getting Parr to feed her on her terms told Christy two things. First, he wasn't planning to kill her, at least not right away. He wanted her healthy and reasonably content until he got more astrology out of her. Second, and perhaps more important, she had some control over the man. She was his prisoner, but he was imprisoned by his own superstitions.

"Hey, lady," Neeley sneered, "ain't you gonna ask Lloyd to get you a six-pack of that diet doctor shit you drink?"

Christy froze. "How do you know what I drink?"

Parr's attention shifted to Neeley. "Yeah, I'm curious too. How you know what she drinks? Are you psychic all of a sudden?"

Caught in the trap of his own words, Neeley looked around helplessly to the others for support that didn't exist. "I saw it in her refrigerator."

"I thought you said you didn't touch nothing but books?"

Neeley squirmed. "I got thirsty so I opened the fridge looking for a beer. That's all, Parr, honest."

"You shithead!" Parr pushed away from the table, stood up, and loomed over Neeley. "You probably left fingerprints for the cops to find."

"Hell, nobody's looking for her, Parr," Neeley said uneasily.

"Not yet, but they will be, thanks to you." He turned and glared at Christy. "That's true, isn't it? Somebody's probably looking for you right now."

She shrugged.

"What about that roommate of yours? Ain't she gonna wonder where you disappeared to?"

"I hardly know her. She moved in last month and keeps to herself. Besides, I go out of town a lot."

"Relatives?"

"My family lives in San Diego," she lied.

Parr's eyes narrowed. "You got a boyfriend that might be missing you?"

Christy was loathe to admit she had no man in her life, even to a drug dealer. It was so easy to lie about everything else.

"We broke up. He wouldn't notice I was gone."

Parr eased back down into his seat. "You don't seem to be much use to anybody except me. Well, that works out fine. I'll just keep an eye on the TV and see if you made the six o'clock news."

Neeley looked at Trimmer, who leaned unsteadily against the sink holding a napkin to the cut on his head. He nodded weakly back.

"Uh, Lloyd, we forgot to tell you. The television hasn't worked in two months."

"What the hell's wrong with it?"

Neeley shrugged. "Don't know. It just stopped working. Nobody watched the damn thing anyway, so we put it in the shed."

"Then go out to the mailbox and get the paper. Maybe there's something about her in the *Kearny Sun*." Parr rubbed his eyes wearily.

"We don't get the paper no more either."

"Why not?" The circles under Parr's eyes seemed to grow blacker.

"Didn't pay the bill, Lloyd." Trimmer picked the chair up off the floor and sat down a safe distance from Parr. "If you don't pay, the paperboy don't deliver. We never read anything but the comics and the police blotter to see who got arrested. Most of the time the papers just rotted on the ground."

Parr glowered at both men. "I guess when the milk gets here, we'll have to see if her picture shows up on the carton," he said through clenched teeth. He pushed the plate of cold fries away, finished with dinner and full of venom. "Get that furniture moved into her room and screw in some light bulbs so she can see."

He picked up a bag from the floor and slid it across the table at Christy. Inside was a ream of paper. "Start working on my horoscope as soon as Joey comes back with your food."

"How far do you want me to go? I can chart you to the year 2050."

Taken aback, Parr muttered, "A couple of weeks' worth, I guess. I don't want to know any more than I can handle." His eyes deadened and he stared past her. "I don't think I've got that much future ahead."

CHAPTER 18

The desk they found had one leg shorter than the others, but she solved that problem by slipping a volume on astrological sex signs under it. It was the only place the book would be useful since Christy loathed the idea of giving Parr clues to his waning sexuality. She used the pink towel from Emilina to cushion the hard wooden back of the chair. A bare bulb glared overhead, but she welcomed the light.

Her stomach growled in protest as she set out paper and pens and proceeded to draw a large circle. She hoped the horoscope would take her mind off hunger until Joey showed up with food.

Before she charted the future, Christy decided to reconstruct Parr's natal horoscope. He thought he had the whole chart, but that wasn't true. Pieces were missing. Wolfe wanted a chart that preyed on Parr's paranoia and superstitions. She'd deleted a few facts from the reading to give Wolfe what he wanted. Now that information would be her weapon against Parr. It was ammunition.

She dissected the circle six times, creating the twelve houses. At home, she had forms with the horoscope wheel already printed on the pages, but creating the circle by hand had a soothing effect.

Starting with the left-hand side, which she labeled with the sign of Pisces, Christy worked her way counter-clockwise around the circle, drawing symbols of the horoscope in order: Aries the ram, Taurus the bull, Gemini the twins, and so on to the water sign, Aquarius.

Working from inside the horoscope where the spokes of the wheel met, Christy numbered the houses in the same order as the signs. She looked up Parr's birth date in the ephemeris and under each planetary symbol she copied a number. Flipping to the current date, she copied a second series of numbers beneath the first. She cleared the table of books and, in astrological shorthand, placed the planets where they belonged on the zodiac wheel.

Christy leaned back against the chair and closely studied the chart of the man who held her life in his drugged grasp. Okay, his intuition was evident—at one time, his perceptions were probably sharply honed. But she knew it took a clear head to handle the barrage of information a receptive mind attracted. Parr's drug-soaked brain would distort, play tricks, cloud his senses. It was a short step from psychic to psychotic. Bullet number one.

Mercury in Parr's chart made him impressionable to occult suggestion. That could be useful. She had a few suggestions she needed to plant in his mind in order to stay out of Blood's reach. If he believed, if he was convinced the messages came from the stars, he would yield to manipulation. Bullet number two.

Venus, found in the same sign as the sun, tipped her off that Parr sought a woman on his wave length, a woman just a little stronger in the occult sciences than he perceived himself to be. It wouldn't take much to play that role. Bullet number three.

A Sagittarian Mars signaled sexist attitudes. Wrapped up in an over-inflated belief in male superiority, Parr acted as though women were beneath him. His treatment of Emilina made that clear. The only woman he'd respect was one he couldn't quite figure out. Christy knew she was smarter than him. She'd just have to stay a step ahead. Bullet number four.

His moon rested in Aries, a strong combination. She'd have to keep an eye on this moon. He controlled people and abused them with his Aries power. His chart showed a marked tendency to manipulate. But the same moon made him temperamental and frustrated. *He'll slip up*, she told herself. *He'll find it harder and harder to control his aggressions, and the drugs will make it worse.* If she worked it right, she might detonate his anger and destroy him without being a casualty. Bullet number five.

The negative side of a Scorpio, Jupiter produced basic, animal urges. Driven to satisfy his needs, he ignored normal human civility. Thoughts came into his head and words erupted from his mouth uncensored. The Scorpion gave false assurance that society's rules didn't apply. A stronger man might fight Scorpio's influence, but not Parr. This was the final bullet.

Slowly, Christy tore the sheet of paper to fine shreds. "I wanted ammunition, Lloyd Parr," she said as she walked to the toilet and watched the incriminating confetti flush away, "and you just gave me an arsenal."

CHAPTER 19

Christy put the final touches on the chart of Parr's natal scope when a key rattled the door lock.

"Come on, Joey's back with your food. And don't try nothing 'cause I got a gun. See?" Neeley lifted up his shirt and showed off a butt of a gun sticking out of his pants.

Christy caught a glimpse of something else. "Is that one of my books?" She saw his face flush crimson.

"I took it from your apartment, but you can have it back. It's a crummy book, and there ain't no sex in it." He jerked it out of his waistband and thrust *Lady Chatterly's Lover* into her hands.

When he turned his back, she wiped the paperback with the towel. She didn't want a trace of him on her book.

❧❧❧

Joey had done well. The bread was seven-grain, the peaches and apricots were ripe enough to dent when she pressed gently with her thumb, and the milk was nowhere near its expiration date.

Christy made a sandwich with bologna and lettuce, but Trimmer insisted on slicing the tomato himself rather than put a knife in her hand. She knew she wouldn't find a clean glass in the cupboard, so she opened the quart of milk and took a swig straight from the carton.

"Cool," Neeley said. "I never saw a chick do that."

"Cool," Joey agreed.

Her mother would be appalled, she thought, as she wiped off a milky moustache. But apparently it scored points with Parr's crew. They seemed a lot more relaxed with Parr out of the room. She sat down across from Trimmer and watched him pensively touch the back of his head, checking his injury. A washcloth with diluted blood stains sat on the table.

"Is your head okay?" She allowed a hint of concern to creep into her voice.

He glared at her. "Would you be okay if you were knocked into a sin—"

"You never shoulda mentioned the dead guy," Joey interrupted. "You knew it would piss him off."

Trimmer picked out strands of hair from the cut. "Everything pisses Lloyd off when he's coming down hard from crank. He's crashing right now. When he wakes up in a day or two, he'll be okay."

"Sonofabitch has a temper," Neeley said, pointing out the obvious.

Neeley seemed eager to talk, so Christy focused on him. "I thought you guys were just trying to scare me. You really haven't killed anybody, have you?"

All three glanced around the table uneasily. Neeley started giggling. "Hell, yes. Lloyd's our own Charlie Manson."

"Shut up, Tim," Trimmer warned.

But Neeley was on a roll. "If we wanted to scare you, we'd tell you the snitch was killed in that room you're sleeping in, sitting on that same mattress. Maybe you'll see his ghost tonight when you do your hocus-pocus stuff."

Christy shivered as she thought of Johnny Blue dying on the ratty mattress. But she decided to put aside her revulsion and use the sliver of knowledge to her advantage.

"You know, now that you mention it, I get the strangest sensation in that room. Does the color blue mean anything to anyone?"

The look of shock which crossed their features was payback for the airless car ride.

"Because that's what I keep picking up," she continued. "And there's no blue in the room, so what does it mean? Probably nothing." She took a bite of her sandwich.

"She really is psychic," Joey whispered to Trimmer.

"Naw, she doesn't know nothing."

Neeley eased his chair away from her. "She knows. Parr was right about her."

"Better watch what kind of vibes you pick up, lady." Trimmer studied her carefully. "If you know too much, we might have to get rid of you."

Christy swallowed. The bread stuck as her throat clenched. She reached for the milk and forced the wad down. "I thought Parr was the boss around here." She made it sound quiet, but threatening. Nobody answered, so she pressed on. "He needs me right now, and you take your orders from him. You can't touch me."

Their silence confirmed everything she said. And, as long as she had their attention...

"It doesn't take much to see things are falling apart around here. I've barely started the horoscope, but the picture is clear. I even saw some very interesting things in his chart concerning you guys."

That last remark caused Trimmer to bolt from the table and pace unsteadily around the kitchen. "You know what? I don't believe in horoscopes or psychic ability or any of that crap."

"Parr believes in it. That's all that matters."

Neeley shifted in his chair, suddenly uncomfortable

with his position and the topic. "I don't believe in this stuff either. So, what did the chart say about us?"

Christy took a bite of her sandwich and chewed contemplatively, as though weighing whether to answer. They waited for her to swallow, and she took her time.

"The horoscope says you're beginning to doubt Parr. Someone else to is ready to step into his shoes. It says Parr better watch his back."

Trimmer leaned toward her and braced both hands on the table. She could smell onions on his breath. "It's Youngblood. He wants to take over because Lloyd's too messed up on drugs most of the time."

"That's not true," Joey protested.

"Yeah, it is, runt, and you know it." Trimmer turned his attention back to Christy. "Lloyd used to be the brains of this outfit, but Blood complains all the time that he uses too much crank and he's burned out." With shaking hands, he retrieved the stub of a marijuana joint from his pocket, slipped it between the teeth of a roach clip, and struck a match.

"Are you gonna tell Lloyd what the chart says?" Neeley was frantic. He looked from Christy to the roach in Trimmer's fingers.

"I can't lie to him. I mean, he knows a lot about horoscopes."

"Not that much." Trimmer handed the joint off to Neeley, who sucked on it like a pacifier. "He just knows what he's told by those dial-a-psychics. Mostly he bullshits about being a Pisces, like it's a big deal. Hell, Neeley's a Pisces and he's no big shit."

Neeley nodded in agreement as he passed the joint to Joey.

"With the horoscope, interpretation is everything. Your lives are on the line if Parr's horoscope says he can't trust the people around him." She peered into their faces to see if they caught her threat.

Trimmer's eyes glinted.

"Here's the deal. If you keep this info quiet—" Trimmer looked at the other men. They both nodded. "—we won't be the ones to kill you, if it comes to that."

Her fate was now in the hands of three men toking on a doobie, and it was the best deal she could make. They offered her a hit on the joint to seal the agreement. Christy declined. She was getting a contact high just sitting in the cloying smoke.

Grabbing a couple of peaches for breakfast, in case they forgot about her in the morning, Christy stood, waiting for an escort.

"We'll keep our word," Trimmer assured her as they walked down the hallway. "But you still need to worry about Blood. If he wants you dead, no horoscope is gonna save you."

With that, the door closed.

CHAPTER 20

The light coming through the green curtains woke Christy from a deep, dreamless sleep. Her head was pillowed on one of her books and the towel served as a sheet to cover the worn and dirty shag carpet. She preferred the floor to the mattress, which seemed even more vile now that she suspected it was Johnny Blue's deathbed. Stretching to work the kinks out of her joints, she pulled herself up to a sitting position and reached for a peach on the desk. Maybe it would kill the rancid taste in her mouth.

The household was quiet except for the occasional bark of the guard dogs. Christy drew up her knees, leaned back against the wall, and let peach juice trickle down her throat as she took stock of the situation. She was alive, unharmed, and fed. Parr's extended nap time gave her an opportunity to sort out the events of the past two days.

Lennie, Sergeant Traynor, and half of the sheriff's department had to be looking for her by now. She wondered if Wolfe was aware of the danger his little prank had put her in. No, she couldn't put all the blame on Wolfe. If she'd followed her instincts and refused to cast the horoscope, none of this would have happened. If she got out alive, maybe she'd give up astrology altogether.

What would Dolly Good say to that? Dolly Good— frizzy hair tied up in a kerchief, a cigarette perpetually hanging from her lower lip with an ash that defied the laws of gravity, flipping tarot cards to read the future— wasn't every grandma like Dolly Good? Christy remembered tales of leprechauns and banshees and the witches of MacBeth, bedtime stories by Edgar Allen Poe read in a thick Yorkshire accent undiminished after four decades in America. Dolly Good said that if she'd settled in Salem a few centuries earlier, there wouldn't be a Good left.

Christy closed her eyes and the confines of Parr's prison dropped away. She was back in Grandma's room, peering in the bottom dresser drawer at Grandma Good's most valued possession: a crystal ball kept in a case lined with red velvet. Christy smiled at the sight of her grandmother peering into the glass orb, expecting visions to appear on cue. A gypsy at heart, if not by descent, her psychic powers seemed to work best at bingo parlors and the horse races, and she was adept at communicating with the dead, or so she said.

But Dolly Good's greatest legacy was her grandchildren.

The Family Talent. According to her grandmother, The Talent always skipped a generation, so Christy and Celeste were next in line. Her sister displayed talent early, when, guided by "voices," she began predicting the future at the age of four. In any other family this would have been cause for concern. Grandma Good took it as a sign of healthy genes.

Grandma questioned the ouija board, dealt the cards, and predicted a brilliant future for the child as a medium. But Catholic school and the Dominican nuns intervened, and eventually Celeste became Sister Catherine, and the voices she heard were most assuredly coming from God.

Aware that she was Dolly Good's one remaining hope, Christy fought against the legacy. She wanted to inherit normal talents, maybe in art or music, or something useful like auto mechanics. While the other kids worked hard at being non-conformists, she melted into the background, saying little about her crazy family, always careful not to attract attention in any way. Yet, despite all of her efforts—or perhaps because of them—astrology blind-sided her and crumbled her defenses. The book that started it all mocked her from its perch on the rickety desk. The first time it beckoned from the dusty book shop in the Tower District, she resisted its pull, resisted being part of Dolly Good's legacy. But there was no escaping. The moment she opened the book and glimpsed the strange, yet somehow familiar symbols, she closed the chapters of denial in her life.

True to form, the family accepted this new strain of occult talent with the same equanimity with which they accepted her sister's calling to the church. Dolly Good declared it was two sides of the same coin.

A headache formed behind Christy's right eye. Even on her best days, her family was too much to think about, and this was not one of her best days. She was surprised to find a tear on her cheek and brushed it angrily away. Tears wouldn't unlock the door or get her clean clothes, and they sure wouldn't break any hearts in the compound. Crying would only get her ridiculed, maybe even killed. Survival was her only goal.

Wolfe got her into this mess, but astrology was the only thing she had to get her out of danger. Her chart predicted a long and productive life. It also indicated romance in the near future, but that looked like a long shot. It never said anything about getting kidnaped by a delusional drug dealer.

She got up, picked up the towel, and went into the bathroom. The face that stared back from the mirror was pasty and haggard. Conditions looked even worse when she slipped her glasses on. Her brown hair hung in limp, stringy clumps and barely responded when she shook it out and combed her fingers through it. Using the tip of the towel, she brushed vigorously at her teeth. She used another section of towel as a wash cloth and scrubbed her face.

Having done her hygienic best, Christy sat down at the desk and took out Parr's horoscope. She studied it again, rehearsing for their next meeting—whenever that might be. His men said he slept for days when he came down off the drugs.

Christy's eye glimpsed a slip of paper peeking out from the pocket of her shorts. It was the Chinese fortune from the Shanghai: *A wise river divides around the rock.* The quote still made no sense, but Christy felt it carried an important message. The fact that it followed her to this Godforsaken place gave the fortune some weight. And Dolly Good taught her, at an early age, to be attentive to omens, portents, and signs. In time, the fortune would reveal its meaning.

CHAPTER 21

Wolfe pulled the crankmobile into a parking space in front of the Dough-Re-Mi pizza parlor and turned the engine off. He leaned back in his seat and watched the slight man in the window working the dough, forearms white with flour up to the elbows. The temperature inside the car rose as it sat in the mid-afternoon heat. Wolfe got out before it became hotter than a pizza oven.

Walking up to the window, he watched the man make several small tosses in the air, the circle of dough stretching each time it became airborne. The man concentrated on the task at hand, twirling the dough on the tips of his fingers, spinning it like a born Italian. Not a bad trick for someone raised on Iranian food and speaking Farsi.

Ahmad Bashood was Wolfe's first drug arrest as a

narc. At the time, he was proud of the collar. Later he realized what an easy target Ahmad had been. The foreign student was as green in the drug game as Wolfe was in drug enforcement. The Iranian could barely recognize cocaine when he sold it to other students—and one undercover detective. Wolfe found a set of written instructions on how to deal coke and a price list when he searched Ahmad. As the student told the detectives, through tears and apologies, he only sold drugs to make ends meet until his allowance arrived from Iran. The kid flipped faster than pizza dough when Wolfe offered him a deal. In exchange for an intro to the supplier, all charges were dropped. Wolfe even found him the job at Dough-Re-Mi.

The dough flattened out to the size of a medium pizza, and Ahmad finished with a flourish, tossing the circle high into the air and closing his eyes as he caught it with deft hands. It was a good trick. Several people stopped to watch, but Wolfe eased his way to the front, close to the pane of glass. A child whined as he blocked her view, but he didn't care. He removed his sunglasses.

Recognition registered on Ahmad's face. The dough stretched elastically over his hands and a knuckle broke through. Wolfe lifted his hand and gave a friendly wave. He pointed to the door, directing Ahmad to meet him inside.

"Ahmad, you running the place now?" Wolfe sat

down on a stool in front of the beer taps and glanced around for the manager.

"Mr. Wolfe, a surprise to see you. The boss is out to lunch. Would you like a cold one, please?"

"Don't tempt me. I'm on duty. Just thought I'd check up on you, see if you're staying out of trouble."

Ahmad looked nervously around at the lunch crowd. "It was a mistake I will never repeat. That is my promise."

"Good. I'm glad we stopped you before you embarked on a life of crime. And now comes the payback. I need a favor."

Ahmad's hands wrung the towel he was holding. "Anything. If I can be of service, it is yours."

"I need that pizza coming out of the oven over there."

Ahmad turned to see his co-worker shoving a wooden paddle under the perfect crust of a pineapple-shrimp pizza.

"That pizza has already been ordered for pick-up. I can make you another just the same, no problem."

"No, I need that one. And I need to borrow your delivery car."

Sweat beads formed at Ahmad's hairline. "Mr. Wolfe, you know I cannot loan the pizza automobile to you. It is against policy."

"The boss isn't around. Who's gonna know unless you tell him?"

"Please don't ask me to break policy. If the pizza is late to the customer, it will be free. I might lose my job."

"This is very important. I'm going to catch a bad guy, and I need a disguise. If the boss fires you, I'll find you another job. I need to borrow a uniform shirt too, one with an American name on it. Got one in the back?" Wolfe got off the stool and pushed through the swinging door to the kitchen, ignoring the "Employees Only" sign. He found a loose, white shirt with the name "Joel" stitched over the pocket. It fit a little snug. He added a paper hat with the Dough-Re-Mi logo. "How do I look?"

Ahmad shook his head sadly. He took the keys off the pegboard and cocked his head toward the back door where the car was kept. Ignoring the protests of his co-worker, Ahmad took the cardboard box containing the pizza and handed it to Wolfe.

"Ahmad."

He looked into Wolfe's strange, green eyes.

"I know I'm asking you to take a chance with your job, but remember, you owe me. Big time."

Ahmad nodded glumly, understanding it was time to pay for his bad choice a year ago.

As he exited out the back door, Wolfe turned. "If it makes any difference, you may be helping me save a young woman's life."

"Thank you, Mr. Wolfe. I will remember that when I am fired."

∾∾∾

Trimmer leaned against the kitchen door and peered through the screen at the dust cloud moving down the driveway.

"Somebody coming," he informed the others.

Neeley got up from the kitchen table and peered out "Better get Lloyd."

"Naw, let's see who it is first. Lloyd gets pissed if he's woke up for something we can take care of."

Trimmer pulled the loose tank top over the butt of his gun. Whatever came down the road, he could handle. As soon as Lloyd and Blood had it out, he'd be second-in-command. Neeley and Joey were already learning to obey his orders.

The car pulled to a stop, and Wolfe got out. He reached into the passenger seat and emerged with a flat cardboard box. Glancing at a slip of paper in his hand and then at the house, he stood in the middle of the driveway, looking perplexed.

"Can I help you?" Trimmer drawled as he opened the kitchen door. Neeley followed, and Joey took a position on the front porch.

"Yeah. You guys order a pizza?" Wolfe stared again

at the slip of paper. "The address is really screwed up. Is this 15150 Rosamond? Did you guys order a pizza about forty-five minutes ago?"

"Naw, you got the wrong address. Get off our property."

"Shit." Wolfe pulled off the flimsy paper hat and wiped his forehead with it. He crumpled it up and tossed it to the ground. "Shit. I gotta do something with this pizza. I've been driving around for twenty minutes trying to figure out where I'm going. The customer probably reported me by now, and the boss will have my head. That's what I get for smoking a doobie on the road." He glanced up at the men. "I can't find this address and I can't deliver cold pizza. You guys want a pizza on the house?"

"What kind?" Neeley stepped forward before Trimmer could stop him.

Lifting the cardboard slightly, Wolfe peered in. "Looks like shrimp and pineapple. What some people will eat, I tell ya."

Joey walked up to take a look. "I like shrimp and pineapple."

"Yeah, but not together. And not on pizza. Pizza should have pepperoni and sausage and extra cheese. That's real pizza," Neeley said.

"So, you guys want this thing, or should I toss it?"

They wanted it. It was food, it was free, and it was

better than chili dogs. Neeley grabbed the box out of his hands.

"Can I hit you up for a glass of water? My throat's kinda raw."

"There's the hose," Trimmer said, pointing to the ground.

"Mind if I use your bathroom?" Wolfe put a pained expression on his face.

Trimmer stood at the threshold and crossed his arms. "Nobody goes into the house."

"No problem. I can take a leak over in those bushes." Wolfe started toward the side of the house.

"Maybe you better leave now."

"He gave us a pizza. Least we can do is give him a beer," Joey piped up. Before Trimmer could stop him, he headed into the kitchen and emerged with a cold brew. "It won't get you in trouble at work, will it?"

"Hell, I'll probably get fired for screwing up the delivery. Might as well have beer on my breath when it happens." He accepted the can gratefully. "My boss was gonna fire me for the beard anyway. He said it was a health risk and wanted me to shave. Hated the ponytail too. Guess he can go screw himself now."

Joey and Neeley pulled out wedges of lukewarm pizza and stood in the sun, cramming half a slice at a time into their mouths. Trimmer glanced warily back at the kitchen.

Wolfe eased himself into the shade. When Trimmer didn't object, he sat wearily on the steps and reached in his hip pocket for a joint. "Mind if I light up?"

"Only if you plan on sharing it," Neeley replied.

Wolfe pretended to take a deep draw then passed the marijuana cigarette on. "Nice place you got here. Quiet."

All three heads nodded, intent on watching the next person take a drag.

"Be a good place to party. Turn the music up loud."

Trimmer looked anxiously toward the house. "Maybe you better get moving, pizza man."

"No problem." Wolfe stood up and dusted off his pants. He headed toward the car. "Keep the roach," he called over his shoulder.

Trimmer watched the car disappear down the road. Maybe it was just a coincidence. He walked over to Joey and Neeley and took a slice of pizza.

"Nice guy," Neeley mumbled between bites.

Joey nodded in agreement.

"Yeah, but Parr would skin us for letting him in the compound." As he removed pieces of shrimp and pineapple, Trimmer couldn't shake the feeling that he'd screwed up. "Throw the box in the field when you're done. No sense in setting Lloyd off. And let's keep this between the three of us, okay?"

Saturn is a test of patience and endurance.

CHAPTER 22

A knock sounded at the door, and Emilina's neon face poked in. Although not a fan of makeup, the sight of Emilina's blue-shadowed eyes and crimson mouth made Christy feel drab. She greeted the woman and greedily noted the "Fun in the Sun" bag bulged.

Emilina pulled a cello wrapped toothbrush out of her satchel. "They feed you yet?"

"I made out a grocery list and they got me some decent food." Christy eyed the toothbrush with relief. "Thanks. I really need to brush."

A cheap plastic hairbrush and a travel-size deodorant emerged from the bag. Finally, toothpaste. Christy snatched up the tube and headed for the bathroom. Her teeth felt furry after two days of no brushing.

Emilina slouched against the bathroom door. "The

guys say Lloyd's crashed for a couple of days. You got lots of time on your hands."

Walking over to the desk, Emilina picked up a volume of astrology and flipped through the pages. "Maybe you could do my chart some more. You could do my future."

Christy studied Emilina's reflection in the mirror. "I'd be more comfortable doing your horoscope in my apartment."

"Yeah, you probably would." She slammed the book closed and jerked her head up. Her eyes were piercing slits. "Are you asking me to get you out of here?"

It was the opening Christy sought. She turned around to face the woman. "It's a perfect opportunity. I don't know what Lloyd wants with me, but if I leave now, things can go back to normal for both of us. None of this ever happened. Come on, Emilina. I've been talking to the guys and they don't like what's going on. I think they'll look the other way if I leave while Parr's asleep. Just leave the door unlocked and create a diversion so I can get to the street."

"Yeah, and who's Parr gonna blame when he wakes up and you ain't here?"

Desperate, Christy clutched at straws of superstition. "I have to get out of here. I think Blood's going to try to kill me. I saw it in the horoscope."

"Maybe you're seeing my death. Because if Blood

finds out I helped you escape, he'll use the needle and send me straight to hell."

The woman's words had a chilling ring of truth. Christy felt her own resolve wilt under Emilina's icy stare.

"You act like you know us—you don't know shit. You think Neeley is stupid, and Joey is too young to be dangerous. I know you've been flirting with the guys. You probably promised them sex if they helped you escape. You think I'm your friend because Lloyd tells me to bring you a few things. Look around, puta. Everybody carries a gun and they protect each other. Maybe they don't like the way things are going right now, but they got no choice. Parr's in charge, that's the way things are down. They risk their life for each other, but nobody's gonna risk their life for you."

Christy had read the woman wrong. She'd appealed to the Virgo side of Emilina and had been stung by the Scorpio.

Christy turned away and walked over to the window to collect her thoughts. Rows and rows of grapevines lay just beyond her reach, freedom separated by a thin plate of glass. Field hands worked the vines. Handfuls of purple grapes spilled into the waiting trays. Two workers, separated from the rest, worked close to the house.

"I hate the fields." Emilina's bitter voice came from behind. "The sun turns you brown like a peasant and the vines cut your hands. I told myself I would do anything to escape. Then I met Lloyd." She pointed a manicured finger at the two men awkwardly wielding the girdling knives. "Those men never cut grapes before. Look how they strip the vines."

As Christy watched, clusters of grapes broke apart in one of the pickers' hands and grapes scattered to the ground.

Emilina shook her head in scorn and turned away from the window. "They won't last a day in the fields."

Christy continued to gaze through the pane. The men were edging closer to the house. If Parr woke up, he'd have a fit. The two inept workers stopped massacring the vines and stared intently in her direction. One raised his hand and waved. Christy jumped at the touch of Emilina's hand on her shoulder.

"Get away from the window. Lloyd will get pissed if he finds out you're flirting with field hands."

CHAPTER 23

After Emilina left, the afternoon crawled by in sweltering anticipation of sundown. Christy settled in the corner with the paperback she'd confiscated from Neeley's waistband.

Lady Chatterly had just had her way with Mellors in the gamekeeper's shack when Trimmer unlocked and opened the door.

"We're gonna let you go outside for a while." He left the door ajar and she stepped across the threshold, surprised at this burst of generosity from her captors. Security in the compound apparently relaxed while Parr slept.

Trimmer led her into the living room and slipped his hand between the folds of heavy avocado-green curtains. He unlatched a patio door and tugged until, protesting, the door moved back on rusted runners.

Christy stepped outside and shielded her eyes from

the bright light. A swimming pool swam into view. "It's a mirage." She blinked, but the water was still there.

"It's real." Trimmer grinned at her. "You can go skinny dipping if you want. Joey won't look."

At the deep end of the pool, Joey Jr. stood on the diving board holding a long pole with a net on the end. He made rhythmic passes through the water, catching debris from the surface. The movement gently rocked the gun stuck in the waistband of his jeans.

"Keep an eye on her, kid," Trimmer called out and disappeared back inside the house.

His attitude struck Christy as cavalier, but it felt good to be out of the claustrophobic room and breathe fresh air. She scanned her new surroundings. The pool was enclosed by a tall chain link fence. The only exit was over the top, or through the house via the patio door or the back exit to the kitchen. On the other side of the fence nearly a dozen vehicles littered the grounds, ranging from a Volkswagen bug to a camper shell. All were in varying stages of disrepair and succumbing to the elements. Some still had tires but most were rusted skeletons with broken windows and doors hanging on hinges. None looked operational.

Out of the corner of her eye, she could see Joey watching her. If there was an easy way to escape, they wouldn't have left her alone with the youngest member of the group. She took careful stock of the teenager as she slipped off her Reeboks and pulled off her socks. It was time to test the waters.

The cement scorched her soles as she hopped quickly to the edge of the pool. One big toe confirmed that the water was blissfully cold, and both feet followed.

It was a weakness. Large, cool, plaster-encased bodies of water were the only things, in Christy's opinion, that made Central Valley summers bearable. Others folks cooled down by river rafting on inner tubes or swimming in irrigation canals, but Christy preferred calm, chlorinated water with no surprises. Several friends had houses or apartment pools, and most were generous about sharing their liquid assets with Lennie and her. But the last thing she expected to find in Parr's backyard was a swimming pool in pristine condition.

Joey kept a careful eye on her as he worked. Even with the gun at his hip, Christy felt more at ease with the boy than with any of the other men in Parr's group. She sensed he was also a prisoner in the compound through the fate of being Joseph Youngblood's son. As Joey emptied the filter basket and replaced the net with a brush attachment, she searched for a way to start a conversation.

"You do a nice job." She moved to let him sweep the steps. "The rest of the house is such a pig sty, I wasn't expecting to find anything like this in the backyard."

Joey gave her a funny look, as though the condition of the house had escaped him until now. He shrugged.

"Lloyd gets pissed if the pool don't look good."

"He doesn't strike me as a swimmer." Christy squinted in Joey's direction, trying to make out the expression of his backlit features.

"Naw, he never gets in it. He doesn't like us to use it either, but sometimes we swim when he's out of town."

"Then what's the point of having a pool? Chemicals must cost a lot of money. Why not let it go like the rest of the house?"

Joey pulled the brush out of the water. "Rich people got pools. It means you made it to the top. The Black Hearts were on top ten years back, they were the gang to be reckoned with, so Lloyd put in the pool. I just turned nine that summer, and my old man brought me over here every day, taught me to dive off that board. Everybody hung out, did their thing. This was a real party house."

He pulled out a test kit as he talked, filled two tubes with pool water, added red drops here, yellow drops there, then studied the results like a Nobel prize-winning chemist.

"You handle the chemicals like an expert. Where did you learn how to do all that?"

"I read books and manuals. Sometimes I go to the pool supply store and talk to the guys that work there. I know as much as they do now."

Christy stepped down to the next level of steps. The water reached mid-thigh, not quite touching the edge of her shorts. Praise had cracked the boy's armor. Now she needed to peek through the opening and find out who she was dealing with. "You know, you could probably start a business of your own, if you wanted. There's a lot of people in Kearny who would pay you to keep their pools looking as good at this one." Christy watched the late afternoon light dance on the surface as she talked. "Maybe someday you could even own your own pool supply store and give people tips on pool care. Ever think of that?"

A flicker of interest crossed Joey's face but was immediately snuffed out. "Yeah, well, I can make more money working with my old man."

"You mean running a meth lab? Why would you want to do something illegal when you have a skill that will make money? You can be more successful than your father without breaking the law."

Christy watched a wall go up. Joey's face hardened and all traces of boyishness disappeared as the nineteen-year-old scowled at her. "You don't get it, do you? My old man is the best cooker in the business. He's got a rep that goes from LA to Redding—maybe even farther. My dad's got respect on the street, and that's not something you can get cleaning swimming pools." He threw down an empty chlorine bottle and reached for the clarifier. Christy was taken aback by the hostility and surprised by the boy's loyalty to his abusive father. "I already know what I'm gonna do with my life," he sullenly informed her. "First, I'm gonna be a mope like Trimmer and Neeley. Then, someday, my dad will train me to be a cooker."

Lab language was only slightly familiar to Christy because narcotics reports rarely crossed her desk. Most of what she knew of lab operations came from Sergeant Traynor's outdated stories. She was surprised to find Parr's men had job titles. "What's a mope?"

Joey gave her a look of exasperation, but she noticed his chest swell slightly as he detailed his world to her. He explained the lab hierarchy: that the "cooker" mixed chemicals from a recipe to get the "cook" going, then the mopes babysat the lab in case the chemical combination was off and the lab blew up. His message was chillingly clear—mopes are expendable. Cookers are not.

His aspiration to a job that had kamikaze career potential appalled her. "And this is what you want to do with your life?" she asked.

"Sure." He took the hose and ran water into the pool. "Someday I hope to have an operation like Lloyd's. Then I'll have money for a nice house and my own pool instead of an old Chevy to sleep in."

This last admission caught Christy short. She looked over the auto graveyard. "You sleep in the cars?"

Joey pointed toward his Chevy of choice. It was a Citation with only one rear window missing. "We all sleep in cars, except my old man. He hangs out at my mom's trailer in Minkler. It's not too bad out here in the summer, but I wish Lloyd would let us sleep in the house when it gets cold."

It was ridiculous. The ranch house looked small from the road but Christy now realized it was much larger. The building forked into two wings, one where they kept her hostage, and the other where Parr slept. She estimated two bedrooms in each wing, possibly three bathrooms in the house. Yet, only Parr slept inside while the others guarded him.

Christy got out of the pool and hurried across the scorching pavement to a small patch of grass near the fence. She stared at the cars while trying to picture Trimmer, Neeley, and Joey bedding down for the night in a junked car. Joey came alongside her.

"This isn't any way to live," she said quietly. "You can do better. You haven't built up much of criminal record, and you can still go back to school and get your diploma. You're a lot smarter than the others, and you're not locked into this lifestyle yet."

Startled, he put down the hose and walked toward her. "How do you know so much about me?"

Christy realized she was repeating info from his sheriff's department file. "I'm p—psychic," she stammered. "I see things."

He weighed her words, his eyes flicking back and forth as if he were balancing logic and loyalty.

She decided to try and tip the scales in her favor. "I may be able to help you, Joey. I know people who will give you a real job where you won't risk getting blown up. I'm talking about a job with benefits and a way to build credit to rent your own apartment and buy a car."

"Yeah?"

The idea of owning a car seemed to strike the right chord. She pressed on. "Sure. You can even use me as a reference after I get out of here. Maybe you could help me—"

"What kind of ideas are you feeding my boy?"

Christy and Joey spun around and found themselves staring into the red-rimmed eyes of Joseph Youngblood. His face was mottled red, either from the heat or his anger. He moved quietly for a large man—she never heard his approach. Christy followed his eyes, which were riveted on Joey's hip. She suddenly realized her hand was only inches from the boy's gun, but she was too numb to react. Blood reached out and slapped his son hard enough to put some distance between the gun handle and her hand. Then he turned his wrath on her.

"Think you're smart, don't you?"

Tary-brown spittle punctuated every word and Christy could smell snuff on his breath. She tried to answer but nothing came out of her constricted throat. It took all of her concentration just to keep breathing. Terrified, she wondered how much of the conversation Blood actually heard.

"Go clean the dog shit out of the yard," he ordered Joey in a low growl. He watched the boy skulk off then turned back to Christy, his eyes ablaze. "Listen to me and listen good," he said, pushing her against the hot metal of the fence. "I don't want to ever catch you talking to my son again. You got that? And don't get any more ideas about escaping. Maybe Lloyd's convinced he needs you, but I could put a bullet in your head without stopping to take a breath." He grabbed her arm and jerked her around like a ragdoll toward the discarded shoes and socks. "Get your stuff. I'm in charge now, and you ain't coming out of that room again until I say."

Blood's steely grip kept her upright as he propelled her through the living room, past a subdued Trimmer, and down the hall to the bedroom. He flung her face down, on the mattress, but she rolled to a sitting position and crab-walked to the farthest end of the bed. Her panic doubled when she realized her glasses were gone. Squinting, Christy stared at the menacing blur that was Youngblood and tried to anticipate his next move. The hazy figure stayed at the door for a few long seconds then slammed it shut and snapped the bolt in place.

Feeling blindly around the mattress, Christy's fingers found her glasses. The frames were bent and they hung lop-sided on her face. She struggled to straighten out the metal, but her hands trembled. All of her efforts were hopeless. She turned the twisted frames over and over in her hands and, without warning, her body convulsed into heaving sobs. She cried with her face buried in the bed to smother the sound. When exhaustion overtook her, she curled up on one corner of the dingy mattress and fell asleep, clutching her glasses.

CHAPTER 24

Christy woke up, disgusted to find her cheek pressed against the soiled mattress. She crawled off the bed and slowly made her way to the bathroom. Yesterday's encounter with Joseph Youngblood left her feeling battered, mentally and physically. A puffy face and swollen eyelids were the aftermath of last night's crying marathon, and the bridge of her nose was bruised where her glasses jammed into her face as she fell. She rinsed the wash cloth in cold water and pressed it against her eyes.

More than anything, she wanted to give her aching body a long soak in a hot tub. She felt filthy after sleeping on the dingy mattress and days spent in the sweltering heat of the room. She smelled bad. She'd been sponging off with the wash cloth and rinsing it out, but now it smelled sour.

Christy glanced over at the tub. The porcelain was gray with dirt and soap scum. Spiders crawled along the ledges and a web went from the faucet handles to the spout. Still, it was tempting. Her hand reached for the rusty hot water knob and she twisted. A trickle of brackish water dribbled out.

Taking a bath meant taking her clothes off. Her hand jerked away from the faucet. Even if Parr was the only one in the house and he was sleeping, he might hear the water running. Christy knew she was being paranoid, but this was definitely the place for paranoia. She left the bathroom.

By mid-morning, it was clear they were ignoring her. Christy strained her ears, trying to gauge the atmosphere in and around the house. It was ominously quiet on the grounds. Even the dogs kept their barking to a minimum. Youngblood's presence filled every corner of the compound and weighted the air with foreboding.

Christy staved off her appetite by drinking lots of water from the bathroom tap. It filled her stomach enough to stop the grumbling. Hunger pangs felt sharper when there was nothing else to think about. She picked up *Lady Chatterly's Lover* and tried to lose herself in the story, but found it hard to concentrate on the words with her mind focused on the other side of the locked door.

There was one other place she could escape to besides the pages of the novel. Often, when life seemed chaotic, Christy found solace in the calculating work involved in charting horoscopes. There was a comfortable, mathematical tidiness to the process, to lining up the planets and tracking their astral journeys. It made sense out of senselessness, and she ended feeling reassured that direction existed in the random currents of life. The universe seemed orderly when she finished, especially her small part of it.

She picked up a blank piece of paper and the ephemeris. The hardest horoscope to cast was always her own. Like a mirror held inches from the face, she was too close to clearly see her own fate. But it was time to delve into her chart and try. She desperately needed some answers, and definitely some hope.

ℰℐℰℐ

It was well past noon when the door opened.

Trimmer appeared anxious as he motioned with his gun for her to come out of the room. She slipped by him and walked down the hall, her senses taking a reading of the atmosphere in the compound with each step. The climate was tense.

He guided her to the kitchen. Neeley sat at the table, half-heartedly picking at a plate of limp French fries. He seemed oblivious to the smell of food that filled the air. Flies checked out the debris of yesterday's dinner which had not been cleared from the table. But a napkin covered a plate containing bread, luncheon meat, and a Diet Dr Pepper. She put together a sandwich and sat down at the table.

"Blood told us not to let you out." Trimmer sounded almost apologetic as he stood at the screen door, gun drawn, watching the yard.

Security was apparently beefed up when Youngblood was in charge. Joey entered the kitchen and reported to Trimmer in quasi-military fashion that he'd completed his rounds of the compound and makeshift auto junkyard. He dropped into a chair in the corner without looking directly at Christy.

Trimmer squinted and trained his eyes on the yard. "We let you out 'cause we figured you had to eat, and Blood's gone for a little while. He chewed our asses good for going easy on you. Don't take this personally, but things are going to come down on you hard from now on."

"Personally" was the only way Christy could take it, and she was about to tell him so.

"I don't think we have any right to hurt her." All eyes turned to look at Joey. He shifted uncomfortably on the chair, but stared defiantly back. "I know my dad says she has no business being here, but we kidnaped her, plain and simple. She didn't have any choice in the matter. It's not her fault."

She'd gotten past his defenses, after all. It helped compensate for the abuse she'd suffered at his father's hands.

Joey stood up. "I don't know if she's a phony like my dad says, or if she really has powers and can tell the future." He gave her a sideways glance. "That's her business. But it's stupid to hurt her just because she did Lloyd's horoscope."

Nobody would look her in the eye, but she sensed they agreed with Joey. A decision seemed to be forming among the three of them, and she knew it directly affected her chances for survival. Loyalties in the group were already strained by the growing rivalry between Parr and Youngblood. Her capture made them doubt their leaders even more.

A wise river divides around the rock. The fortune cookie suddenly made sense. These men would be her route around Parr and Youngblood.

"We got company," Neeley announced as he stood and reached for his gun. Before Christy could look through the kitchen door, Trimmer grabbed her upper arm and propelled her down the hallway to the room.

ℰᔆℰᔆ

Gravel crunched under the heels of her strappy sandals. "Come on, take it slow, act casual," Lennie cautioned herself between clinched teeth as she teetered toward the ranch house. When Wolfe failed to infiltrate the compound armed with a pizza, Lennie decided it was time to take matters into her own hands. She spent all morning abusing the computer until it spit out Parr's address, and a sudden "toothache" got her out of the substation by noon. She had no clear plan of attack, but improvising had always worked in the past. She trusted her instincts.

The Volvo had lots of practice breaking down, but today it needed a little assistance. Just before locking up and leaving her car on the deserted county road, Lennie hunkered down in the front seat and wrestled her bra loose. She stuffed it in the glove compartment, along with the distributor cap.

As she walked down the long driveway, the pitbulls chained around the tree strained to get a piece of her. The men at the doorway had the same lathered look. Pretending to stumble, Lennie bent at the waist and felt her short-shorts ride up her rump. She examined her shoe for phantom pebbles. The V-neck gaped open on cue to reveal her forty double Ds.

Allowing the men enough time to get a good look, Lennie pulled herself up to her full five feet, eleven inches, threw her red mane back, and flashed a hundred-watt smile. "How you guys doing?"

They were staring at her forty-inch chest and doing

just fine. The two older scuzzballs reminded Lennie of her ex-husband's friends. Her ex was a doper, so she knew the type well. The baby-faced one looked redeemable, but the gun showing through his T-shirt meant he was on his way.

"My car crapped out down the road, and I need to use a phone to call a tow." She heard her voice jitter from nerves and quickly covered it with a throaty laugh. As an extra diversion, she tucked her shirt down into her shorts until it stretched tightly across her chest. She demurely used two fingers to wipe nervous sweat from her cleavage.

"Don't you carry a cell phone?" asked Trimmer.

"Battery's out. Probably couldn't get a decent signal out here anyway."

Neeley took the bait. He stepped forward and invited her in to use the phone, cutting off the protests of the other two.

Entering the kitchen, a fetid stench hit Lennie's nose. Flies dive bombed open containers of food, and a mountain of dirty dishes completely buried the sink.

She half-hoped her theory was wrong, that her fastidious roommate wasn't anywhere near this filth.

Neeley moved in close, his eyes never leaving the logo on her T-shirt. "The phone's right there, on the wall. Can I get you a beer? Some weed?"

"A beer would be great. I'll take a rain check on the other."

Joey stood at the kitchen door, wild-eyed and nervous. "You're not supposed to let anybody in. My dad might come back."

"Or the boss might wake up," Trimmer chimed in.

"Get a grip, you guys. She just needs to use the phone."

The phone was ancient, avocado green, and rotary dial. Clutching her auto club card, Lennie dialed the number for the time and leaned seductively against the wall. She took the beer Neeley handed her and made a show of rubbing the cold can on her neck, letting the condensation drip south. As she gave the Time Lady all the details for picking up her car, her ears listened for sounds from the back of the house and her eyes cased the kitchen.

She spotted it—hidden behind the garbage can, in the pile of litter that overflowed the bag. The Diet Dr Pepper can peeked out, half covered by fast food bags. This didn't strike her as the type of household where diet soda would be on the grocery list. It was clear proof that they had Christy.

She concluded the phony call and hung up. "You guys have been more help than you know. I wish I could find a way to pay you back." She peeked her head through the doorway and down the hall. "I need to use your bathroom. Which door is it?"

Joey moved to block the hallway. Neeley turned pale.

"Bathroom doesn't work, the plumbing's messed up." Trimmer pushed his hair away and his eyes dared her to call him a liar.

"That's okay. The tow should be here soon. I'll go wait by the car."

Lennie walked slowly down the driveway, acutely aware of three pairs of eyes watching her retreat. Back at the car, out of their sight, she replaced the distributor cap, jumped in, and cussed as her thighs touched the hot upholstery. Pushing pain aside, she purposely stalled the car a few times for effect then eased it onto the asphalt.

Her hands danced around the burning plastic of the wheel, steering with only her fingertips. She reached in the glove compartment and located her cell phone. She'd call Traynor and Perrelli and tell them she had concrete evidence proving Christy was in the house. Then maybe they'd get off their butts and send in the SWAT Team.

Concentrating on pushing the Volvo to maximum speed and dialing the phone at the same time, Lennie didn't glance into her rear view mirror until the grill of the pickup truck filled her back window. There was plenty of room to pass and not a soul on the road, but the truck bore down. It had to be those cranksters following her, checking her story, maybe coming to get what she dangled. She dropped the cell phone to the floor. The car wouldn't go any faster, no matter how frantically she pressed on the gas pedal.

She never saw the pot hole. Her fingertips flew off the wheel and she lost control. The Volvo shot off the road and hit a grape post, knocking her unconscious.

Communication, under the influence of Mercury, brings both good news and bad, gossip and information.

CHAPTER 25

Lennie heard male voices swirling in the dark confusion around her, muted and angry. She struggled with memory and emerged with the notion that the men might be dangerous. Without moving, she took stock of the situation and found she was buck naked, covered by a thin shirt and a cool sheet—not a good sign. She debated whether to open her eyes or play possum awhile longer.

She inhaled slowly, her nose tickling from a sharp odor. It was a smell she knew from childhood, a dreaded mix of alcohol and disinfectant…

"Am I in a hospital?"

Four men clustered around the bed turned in unison to stare down at her. She struggled to bring them into focus. Two were dressed for field work, one wore a suit and tie, and one wore the olive green of a deputy sheriff.

A man in a white lab coat pressed through the crowd.

He pulled her eyelids apart and bent close to shine a light in her eyes. He smelled like wintergreen chewing gum and Aspen cologne. "Ms. Watkins? How do you feel? Do you know where you are?"

"Either I'm in a hospital, or else you're dressed real funny for the substation." She pulled away from the light. "Is that Sergeant Traynor behind you?"

Traynor edged his way along the side of the bed until he stood next to the doctor. "I'm here, Lennie."

"Everything's fuzzy in my head. How did I wind up here?" She struggled to sit up.

The doctor put a warm hand on her shoulder and pushed her back to the pillow. He was stronger than he looked. "You were in a car accident. Do you remember where you were this afternoon?"

Lennie shook her head. It hurt.

"Meet Agents Espinoza and Ybarra." Traynor stood back and motioned toward the farm workers, who gave a friendly wave. "They were on surveillance when you parked your car and walked up Lloyd Parr's driveway. They ran your license, and dispatch told them you worked for us."

One of the men stepped forward. "We tried to stop you for questioning, but I guess we scared you. You lost control of your car and ran off the road. Next thing we knew, you were knocked out and we radioed for paramedics."

"Your car's totaled, by the way," added the second agent.

The Volvo was a piece of junk, but now she had no transportation at all. Insurance wouldn't pay for a scooter, much less a new car. Lennie couldn't remember the crash, but bits and pieces of the afternoon filtered into her head. The truck following too close, the blistering heat of the steering wheel, a pot hole the size of a crater. And one more thing.

"I've got the proof we need that Christy's in the house."

That got everyone's attention, especially the Suit, who had not been introduced. "Did you see her?" he now asked.

"No, but I saw a Diet Dr Pepper can in the garbage." She watched a skeptical look cross the man's face. "You don't get it. That's the only soda Christy drinks. Tell him, Sarge."

"She's right." Traynor looked embarrassed, but stood by Lennie's sleuthing. "I realize this is not much to go on—"

"That's an understatement. You're asking me to down a ten-month investigation based on evidence of a soda can. I can't wait to see the judge's face when I use that as probable cause for a search warrant."

"Who is this jerk?" Lennie asked no one in particular. "Listen, mister, don't knock yourself out. It's only my best friend being held prisoner in that pigsty for the last three days."

"Then why don't you give us some information we can use?"

They squared off, matching angry looks and tempers. "If you've got questions, fire away." Lennie crossed her arms and dared him to dispel her theory.

"First of all, how did you penetrate the Parr residence?"

"I was invited in. I told them I had car trouble and needed to use the phone."

"How many men were guarding the place?"

"Three."

Agent Ybarra pulled a pad out and wrote as fast as she answered.

"Were they armed?"

"I saw the outline of a gun under one man's shirt. I assumed the other two had guns."

"Were you armed?"

Lennie drew a bead on the man. "You might say that. I took my bra off and flashed them."

He momentarily lost his official tone. "This tactic worked?"

"Works on most men." She looked the suit up and down. He was probably the exception. "Great-Grandma Dobbs taught me when all else fails, use your charms. Those happen to be my best charms."

Flustered, he continued the debriefing. "Can you describe the men?"

Lennie gave complete descriptions, adding that the one who seemed to be in charge addressed the younger boy as "Joey."

"The leader she describes doesn't sound like Parr," Agent Espinoza said.

"They also mentioned somebody sleeping in the back. They called him 'the boss.' And the young kid said something about his dad coming back. He seemed real keyed up about it."

Ybarra filled the paper with notes. "She's talking about the Youngbloods. So far, her story checks out against our surveillance."

They asked about the floor plan of the house, and Lennie told them what little she knew from her vantage point in the kitchen. But something tugged at her memory.

"At one point, I looked around the corner and down the hallway, and that shook everybody up. All I saw were a couple closed doors and a bathroom at the end. I told them I had to use the toilet, and they said the plumbing was messed up. But you know, I could've sworn I heard a toilet flush. It seemed to come from the door with the padlock on it."

As soon as the words left her mouth, she knew what she had just implied. So did everyone in the room. But implication was still not proof, not in the mind of the man asking the questions.

"It's not much to go on without visual evidence that the Bristol woman is inside the house."

"What does it take to get you people in gear?" Lennie yelled. "Do you need a set of eight-by-ten-inch glossies before you make a move? Somebody get me some clothes. I'm going back to Parr's place and haul her out of there by myself."

She tried to swing her legs over the edge of the bed, but they wouldn't budge. Lifting the covers, Lennie peeked in to check the problem. Her right leg was encased in a cast.

"Get me out of this thing!"

The doctor rushed to restrain her. "You've suffered a concussion and a fractured tibia. It's not feasible for you to leave right now."

"You heard the doc. You're going to stay right here, out of our hair for the whole weekend." The man stared coldly at Traynor. "I'll even post a guard for her protection—and ours. With your office assistant out of the way, maybe we can do our job." He turned on his heel and left.

"Who the hell does he think he is?" Lennie asked.

"Percy Monroe, head of Kearny DEA," Espinoza replied.

The Big Guns. Lennie bit her lower lip hard to keep from crying out from frustration. All she wanted to do was help Christy, but instead she'd made a mess of things, and a fool of herself.

"Is there anything else you want to tell us? Anything we can do for you?" Ybarra waited, pen ready.

"Yeah. My bra's probably still in the glove compartment. I'd hate to lose it, I had it broken in just right. Since you guys made me crash the car, maybe you could go find it for me. Black, lacy, size forty-double-D. You can't miss it."

With a grin, both agents promised they'd make it a priority. Then they left.

"You aren't really going to hold me in this room all weekend, are you?" She looked from the doctor, whose name tag read "Dr. T. Brant," to Sergeant Traynor.

"Where you do expect to go with your leg out of commission and no car?" Traynor held up an overnight bag. "I stopped by your place and had your landlady pack a few things to make your stay more comfortable."

The bedside phone rang, startling the three of them. Dr. Brant handed the receiver to Lennie. Mrs. Alcorn's chirpy voice came across the line.

"Lennie, there's a man with a telegram for you. Would you like me to sign for it and read it?"

"Yeah, go ahead.

"Oh, dear. Your Aunt Leonida died. Bad things seem to come in threes. First, Christy disappears, then you wreck your car, and now a death in the family. Oh, but here's good news. The estate lawyers would like you to contact them immediately regarding your inheritance."

Aunt Lennie? Inheritance? Lennie's head swam. She hadn't thought of her maiden aunt in years. The woman lived in the Seattle area and worked all her life for an eccentric coffee importer. Lennie never expected to be heir to anything besides a truly awful first name. She hoped the windfall would be enough to buy a new car.

It was all in the horoscope. "Someone will die," Christy had told her. Now, with Christy's life at stake, Lennie's own good fortune decided to kick in.

She dropped the receiver as dizziness swept over her. Closing her eyes, she took a deep breath and sank back into the pillow. Dr. Brant rushed to her side and took her wrist to check her pulse.

Lennie could not resist peeking. Sure enough, there was no ring on his finger.

Instant response to her needs. She liked that in a man.

CHAPTER 26

It was nearly ten in the evening when Parr sent for her. Christy grabbed her notes then followed Trimmer to the living room where Parr waited. He sat in the Naugahyde lounger with the patio windows closed and the heavy curtains drawn shut. A fan on high speed blew directly on him.

Something seemed different about the man, but Christy couldn't put her finger on it. Drawing closer, she noticed his hair was freshly washed and still a little damp. He'd combed it down in an attempt to control the natural waves. Was that mousse? His beard was trimmed, and his clothes were wrinkled but clean. He appeared rested and alert. The black lacquer box of drugs sat on top of the bookshelf, well out of reach.

Parr pointed a finger at the cracked footstool at his feet. Instead, she chose a hard-backed chair and positioned it beside him under the narrow spill of light from the lamp. He motioned for Trimmer to leave the room.

Christy gave Parr the drawing of the horoscope wheel, and he held it carefully between shaking fingers. He looked pensive, almost afraid of it, and his fear made her stronger.

"I'll start with the long-term planets in your chart," she began. "Pluto is currently ten degrees into your ninth house, a third of the way through a twenty-year span. The ninth house indicates a journey, but not necessarily to a place. It can also mean a spiritual journey, and the destination could be within yourself. However you choose to define this transit, you need to realize it's going to take many years to complete." In her mind, Christy saw a trip to prison and a life sentence without parole, but she kept the reading vague enough for Parr to supply his own interpretation.

"Pluto is the planet of upheaval, so this journey is going to be very hard. You'll get a break when Jupiter joins Pluto. Jupiter means positive energy, but it only stays twelve months. That happens next year."

Christy's voice slipped into a soothing, hypnotic cadence, what Lennie called her "fortune-teller voice." Parr's breathing became rhythmic, and he swayed slightly as he followed her words.

"Neptune and Uranus are moving together through the universe right now. In your chart, they're halfway through the eleventh house. These planets are guiding strangers into your life. They're coming soon, judging from the positions of your short-term planets."

Parr pulled free of the web spun by her voice and became alert. Did the term "SWAT Team" cross his mind, too? She hastened to put a positive spin on the prediction.

"Neptune and Uranus are benefic planets, so I see opportunity and the realization of goals during this transit. Help comes from an unexpected visitor offering a solution to your current problems."

Parr's eyes glazed over. The stars had seduced him enough for her plan.

She took a deep breath. "That's the good news. Now here's the bad."

Parr snapped back into focus.

She concentrated on keeping her voice steady "Saturn is close to the end of its cycle in the twelfth house. Saturn's had some bad effects on you over the last two years, causing depression and unreasonable fears. You've been hiding away to avoid thinking and making decisions—according to your chart," she hastily added. She was relieved when he nodded in agreement.

"It's not your fault that Saturn makes you act this way, but your behavior has made someone close to you very angry. I'm afraid you can't trust that person anymore. Do you know who that could be?"

Parr's eyes narrowed with paranoia then widened as he recognized his enemy. "Blood!"

Christy bowed her head. She neither agreed nor disagreed with his conclusion but glanced through her bangs and saw his face register pain, regret, and, finally, anger.

"The horoscope's right. I've seen this coming for a long time." His eyes were hard and flat, the color of gun metal. "Little by little, he's taken over my operation. I know what he's planning, I can read his mind. I can see into his soul. He wants all this for himself." Parr looked possessively around the living room. The mismatched furniture and garbage seem to hold value to their owner. "Blood was like a brother when we rode together. Now he's turned the men against me. Trimmer and Neeley don't follow my orders anymore. And he's training his boy to cook meth, probably going to promote him to second-in-command after he gets rid of me. Make it a family operation."

Spittle stained the corners of Parr's mouth white and his hair worked free of the mousse as he ran his fingers through it. He reminded Christy of a rabid dog. In his ranting, he seemed to have forgotten her.

"It was Blood who ordered the hit on the snitch. I told him the kid couldn't touch us, but Blood said we had to send a message to the narcs. He put the heroin in the needle, even used his own kit. But he's too smart to get his hands dirty. Trimmer and Neeley gave Johnny Blue the hot shot. They did it right here in my house. Now I gotta live with his ghost."

Confession might be good for the soul, but murder was more than Christy wanted to hear. She already had enough information to put everyone in the compound behind bars for twenty-five to life. *If* she could find concrete proof they killed Wolfe's confidential informant. And *if* she made it out alive.

But Parr wasn't finished unloading his anger. "Blood was pissed that I had Emilina. He hated her, said she was taking my mind off business, and business always came first. I even thought about marrying her when she got knocked up. But Blood told me she was sleeping with the mopes, so I beat her until she lost the baby. I never even asked her if it was true. After that, I made everybody sleep outside, so they wouldn't get any ideas of taking my women."

Parr as a victim. It didn't make Christy like the man, or even sympathize with him, but it made him slightly more human. He'd had feelings once, at least for Emilina, but his trust in Youngblood snuffed them out.

Seeds of doubt, that's all she meant to plant with the horoscope. But now she knew the relationship between Parr and Youngblood was rotting at the roots long before she ever entered the picture.

The rest of the horoscope was anticlimactic. Parr's interest waned while he listened to her explain that Venus indicated it was a good time to do business and Mercury encouraged him to look after his investments. The man who would assist the Black Hearts was coming very soon, before the end of the month, according to the sun in the sixth house. Parr roused himself at the mention of the stranger. Christy assured him that he would have the energy and stamina for the encounter ahead.

When she finished the reading, Parr rose from the lounger and walked toward the cabinet. He reached up and took the lacquer box off the top shelf. Across the room, a shadowy figure filled the entry.

Blood stood at the door. He nodded to Parr and glanced at the box of meth. His upper lip curled in undisguised contempt at the sight of the horoscope wheel and the handwritten pages. He glared at Christy. She teetered on the edge of the chair, feeling like a skittish canary.

"I got someone here I want you to meet." He stood aside and a tall figure edged through the doorway.

"Shake hands with Trace Malin," Blood commanded Christy. "He just got out of the Oregon State Pen."

CHAPTER 27

Trace Malin scrutinized Christy from a six-foot-three stance. He leaned in for a better look and a short, brown ponytail slipped over one shoulder. A gold stud on the opposite earlobe balanced his narrow face. His gray-flecked moustache overshot his upper lip and dribbled down the corners of his mouth.

"How ya doin'?" he asked her.

Christy wasn't doing well. She managed a weak nod in greeting.

Trimmer and Neeley eased into the room, trying to go unnoticed in the shadows.

"Trace says he got out of prison early," Blood explained.

"Yeah, I got time off for good behavior, and they needed the bed space for some serious offenders." Trace winked at Christy. "I barely crossed the county line when

I heard from the dudes at the Hog Jowls that Blood was askin' about my welfare."

"See? We got a problem here in the compound, Trace." Blood walked over and stood behind Christy. "This lady's an astrologer. She says you asked her to do Lloyd's horoscope while you were in prison. Is that true?"

Deathly silence filled the room as everyone waited for the answer. Malin's cool, blue eyes studied Christy, and she braced herself for his denial.

"Well, I'll tell you, Blood, she doesn't look like a lady who lies."

His answer caught Youngblood off guard. Trace Malin, the ace in the hole, turned out to be a wild card. Christy felt the first stirrings of hope. The game wasn't over yet.

"Are you telling me her story's true? Then where the hell did you get Lloyd's birth date from? I don't recall you sending any birthday cards, Trace."

"Why? Just because I never sent you one?" Trace shuffled over to the couch and sat with his long legs splayed on either side of the coffee table. "Sometimes I use Lloyd's birthday, like for instance, when cops stop me for speeding. An extra birthday comes in real handy. Hell, I even tried to use it in Oregon. You know, they got some pretty sharp cops up that way. It didn't take them long to figure out I was lying this last time." He winked at Christy and gave her a rakish grin. "I reckon they got a good fingerprint system with computers and all."

Youngblood looked from Trace to Christy and back to Trace. "Why'd you pick an astrologer in Coronita if you were in Oregon?" He crossed his arms and waited for a reply.

"All these questions are starting to work on my nerves, Blood." Trace rubbed his eyes, as though he had a headache. "I thought you guys would be happy to see me after four years. I don't even have a beer in my hand, and you're giving me the third degree. Damn little hospitality left around here. Not like the old days."

Parr motioned for Neeley to get their guest a beer.

"You ain't answered my question, Trace."

Malin looked into Youngblood's narrowed eyes. "I heard about this lady from a buddy around here who's into the astrology scene, like Lloyd here. He gave me the address and phone number." Malin took the beer that Neeley offered and used the edge of the coffee table as a bottle opener. He chugged half of the contents before reluctantly pulling away. "Damn, it's hot in here, Lloyd. You oughta put in air conditioning. A swamp cooler, at least."

"Your friend got a name?"

"Give it a rest, Blood," Parr ordered. "You got your answer. Her story checks out."

Trace continued to drink his beer, studying the faces

of his former gang and finally settling on Christy's. "Say Lloyd, what's she doing here anyhow? Did she give you some bad information from the Milky Way?"

Before Parr could reply, Blood said, "He liked your present so much he decided to kidnap her."

"Kidnaping, huh?" Trace pulled at one side of his moustache. "I do believe that's a federal offense. You folks are sure coming up in the world!" In a more serious tone, he asked Parr, "How long has she been here—"

"Long enough to know too much," Youngblood interrupted again. "I keep telling Lloyd we got to get rid of her before the law starts sniffing around."

Parr gave his lab man a withering glare. "All those fumes have fried your brains. You're so hinked up, you think the grape pickers are SWAT commandos coming to bust us."

It was hard to listen to herself being discussed as if she were invisible. This strange turn of events engulfed Christy in a panic. She wanted to get back to the room so she could work out the puzzle of Trace Malin. He was such an adept liar that she found herself believing his corroboration of her story, which she knew was pure fiction. If she couldn't leave the room, then it was better not to draw attention to herself. She hunkered down in the plastic chair and listened for more clues.

Stung by Parr's implication that he was paranoid, Blood retaliated. "Kidnaping is all they can bust us for these days. It's been over eight months since we've done a cook. Tell him, Lloyd. Tell him how we lost all our runners and buyers while you stayed stoned and ran up the phone bill calling those phony astrologers."

Everyone braced for Parr's reaction. But Malin's patter broke up the silence.

"Oh, I'll bet you have lots to tell me, but I gotta have another brew. Why don't you open some windows in this stinkin' place? I forgot the Valley is hotter than hell this time of year, or I wouldn't have come back in August. Oregon State Pen was hell too, but at least there was a cool breeze."

While Neeley went to fetch another beer, Trimmer asked, "We heard you were in Oregon. What were you doing time for, Trace?"

Malin swatted away the question like a pesky fly. "Some lumberjack took offense of my language in front of his girlfriend, so I roughed him up a little. Then the cops showed up and got me on a concealed weapons charge. And resisting arrest. Oh, and they found a few measly bindles of cocaine in my pocket. It was next to my stash of weed. They just don't like us Californians."

Once he had the second beer in his hand, Malin reeled in his long legs and stood up to take center stage. "You guys haven't asked me why I came back, but it wasn't because I missed your ugly faces. I got the message Blood was looking for me, which was a coincidence because I just heard some scuttlebutt about the Black Hearts. Word on the cell block was that this team stopped operating. Whoa! I'm sitting in prison wondering if everybody in the gang got busted, got wasted, or got married."

He held the floor like a midway carny. Christy even found herself drawn into his performance.

"Then, through the grapevine, I heard the lab was shut down because there's no ephedrine. I guess they made the chemical illegal while I was put away."

"That's a fact," agreed Parr. "It's still legal in parts of Europe though. The Germans are making the stuff and shipping it to Mexico. We gotta have it to cook, but the Mexicans control all the ephedrine coming into the States. Right now, it's scarcer than cocaine and just as expensive."

"Yeah, I heard the border brothers were pushing you out of business. How'd they get a toehold?"

Blood filled Trace in. "After the big freeze last year wiped out the orange crop, people were hurting. That's when the Mexicans moved in. They set up labs all around the Valley, got a recipe, and started cookin'. Lots of their labs blew up, and their product's coarse as oatmeal, but they're makin' money. And they went and dried up the market on ephedrine."

Trace leaned against the bookshelf and looked over the group. "I can see you've had a run of bad luck. But now your worries are over. I'm here to put you back on top, get your lab cookin' again, and mow down the competition. I got a way to make pink meth, lemon meth, and some smooth peanut butter meth that will melt in your nose, not in your hands."

"How you gonna do all that without ephedrine?" Trimmer wanted to know.

Malin whirled around and pointed a bony finger at the mope. "Glad you asked. When I was kicking back in the Big House, I met some interesting people. Most interesting of all were these four Colombians from Bogota. Not the brightest bunch in the world, though. They were picked up with forty kilos of coke running the I-5 pipeline. Oregon police stopped them for a broken tail light and doing ninety-five in the slow lane. The rest is history."

He swigged the rest of the beer and motioned for Trimmer to fetch another. With a fresh one in hand, he continued. "But these guys weren't just your run-of-the-mill drug runners. No, these particular mules were part of a pack that works for a Colombian honcho by the name of Luis Rojas Mondragon."

There was an audible intake of breath around the room at the mention of the name.

Parr exhaled. "The Dragon!"

Malin nodded. "The Firebreather himself. And here I am in prison hanging out with his men. Talk about luck."

Malin wiped his forehead with the cold bottle. "Damn, Parr, turn that fan this way. I'm working up a sweat telling this story, and I haven't gotten to the good part."

Christy watched as Parr got up and turned the fan toward Malin. The stranger seemed to have a mesmerizing effect on the group that went beyond his colorful narration. Even Blood—who seemed to have reservations about Malin's credibility—was caught up in the tale of Malin's prison exploits. Christy studied the man as he worked the room like a seasoned performer. He'd lied about contacting her. How much of this story was true and how much was fabrication?

With cool air blowing in his direction, Malin continued. "I told these Colombians about my life with you lab rats and they relayed it back to the Dragon. He was more than a little interested. Seems cocaine is getting too hot to handle and is too much work to produce. I guess every agency in the world is down in Columbia trying to control the traffic. So, the Dragon is looking for a new line of work, something that doesn't cross international borders and can be manufactured, not grown. In other words, the Dragon wants to get into the business of making meth, and he likes what he hears about the Central Valley."

"You call this good news?" Youngblood emitted a harsh laugh. "You're telling us another amateur is gonna set up shop and in our backyard, and we're supposed to be happy about it? You shoulda kept your mouth shut in prison and left the bean-eaters alone."

Malin gave Youngblood a look of pity. "There you go again, Blood, firing off a round before you take aim. This Dragon wants to run a lab, but he doesn't know shit about it, and neither do his people. All they know is cocaine. They want to see a lab in action, get the feel of the operation, and I convinced them that nobody could do a better cook than Joseph Youngblood and Lloyd Parr."

"Except we ain't done a lab in a long time and don't have any ephedrine to do one," Neeley reminded him.

"Aha! See? That's the good news," Malin said, whirling around to face Neeley. "The Dragon just happens to have a stash of ephedrine in his possession, more than we could use in a dozen cooks. He has what we need, and we have what he needs, the recipe for the best methamphetamine around. The man is ready to negotiate."

"How do you know this?" asked Parr.

"Because I've been talking to the Dragon. Face to face."

A stunned silence filled the room. Malin turned to Parr. "He wants to meet with you as soon as possible," he said with feigned nonchalance. "Think you can pencil him in on your social calendar for tomorrow night? Say, cocktails and drug deals at eight?"

CHAPTER 28

It was two a.m. Neeley and Trimmer had driven Trace to a motel for the night. Christy's eyelids were drooping. The surge of adrenalin over the sudden appearance of Trace Malin left her exhausted in its wake. She continued to sit propped up in the corner, the horoscope neatly folded in her lap, and waited for Parr to give a sign that he was done with her for the night.

But Parr's attention was riveted on Youngblood. The two squared off at either end of the living room, tensed for battle. Malin's command performance had opened old wounds between them and freshened the new ones inflicted on Parr by the horoscope.

"When did you ever trust anything Malin said?" Youngblood asked Parr. "You always called him the biggest bullshitter in the gang when we rode together."

"You're just pissed off. Hell, this woman had no way

of pulling his name out of thin air. Any idiot woulda figured that out. But you brought him here to prove you're right. Only you're wrong." Parr took a hit of meth and rubbed the loose powder from his nose.

"Take it easy on that stuff. We're down to a few ounces," warned Youngblood.

"Pretty soon we'll have a stash to keep us high and happy for a year. Maybe I'll use the money for some air conditioning, like Trace said. Too damn hot in this place. Maybe get some decent furniture too."

Youngblood looked warily at Parr. "You're rushin' into this deal too damn fast. We lose track of Trace up north a couple years, and now he shows up, says he's got a big deal for us with the Mondragon cartel. It don't feel right."

"Coincidence, that's all."

"I don't believe in coincidence," Youngblood shot back.

Parr looked his cooker up and down. "What the hell you do believe in?"

"Mixing it up with Mexicans is a bad move. We never counted on outsiders to run our labs. We kept our business to ourselves. You're gonna let a wetback come inside the compound, sit down over beers, and work out a business deal? It ain't right." Having said his piece, Youngblood dropped heavily on the sagging couch and put his workboots up on the coffee table.

Parr glared at the boots. "The Dragon's not Mexican. He's Colombian."

"Same difference."

"She told me the Dragon was coming. She told me last night." Parr stood up and lunged for the horoscope on Christy's lap. She recoiled into the back of the chair as he snapped the folded pages open and shook them at Youngblood. "You don't believe, but I tell you she sat here and told me this was gonna happen."

"She made a lucky guess, that's all."

"You mean, like a coincidence? You don't believe in coincidences!"

"No," Youngblood snarled. "She's just a damn fortune teller. Did she tell you a tall, dark stranger was coming into your life? Get a grip, Lloyd. Are you gonna listen to the stars or your read your palm or a bunch of cards to make decisions? In this game, all you can count on is yourself and your partners."

Parr gave him a hard look. "I'm beginning to think I can only count on myself."

Youngblood bristled. "How am I supposed to take that?"

"Take it any way you want. But don't try and convince me your conscience is clean when I know otherwise."

Christy didn't know whether Parr meant to look her way or not, but the damage was done.

Youngblood honed in on her with the deadly aim of

a laser. "That bitch is planting bitter seeds, Lloyd. She's gonna tear us apart. I can take care of the problem if you let me. I can do it tonight. Just say the word and that's one less thing you have to concern yourself with."

Christy knew he meant it. In his eyes glowed the instincts of a killer, like a dog that'd tasted blood and craved more.

"Well, thanks, Blood. But when I see a problem, I'll take care of it. There's no problem here, except maybe your attitude. I didn't need anyone to tell me what's been going on behind my back."

Parr leaned forward in the lounger and lowered his voice to a soft growl. "You're a damn good cooker, Blood, but you're not the brains of this outfit. I was in the lead spot when we rode and I've stayed at the head of the formation all these years because I've got leadership qualities. Says so in my horoscope." He leaned back into the padded Naugahyde. "Anyway, what makes you think I'm so anxious to work for the Colombians all of a sudden? Thought you knew me better than that."

"What are you leading up to, Lloyd?"

Parr's eyes glinted like cold steel. "We need that ephedrine, no argument there. But there's no contract says we have to give them anything back."

"You talking about doing a rip? On the Dragon? That's like signing your own death warrant." Youngblood ran his hand through greasy hair. "I hear they're worse than the Mafia, and they have more ways of torture than a man has body parts."

"What if we did a bad lab?"

Youngblood thought it over. "Well, yeah, we could do that. We might have to sacrifice one of the mopes to pull it off, but it's a possibility. And you know," he added, warming to the idea, "if we did decide to kill Mondragon, we could throw the body in the blaze and let the Colombians think it was an accident. Then they wouldn't retaliate. That's a helluva a plan, Lloyd."

Murder. It was a "helluva plan." A dangerous, foolhardy, cold-blooded plan. Christy hadn't seen it coming, not in any part of the horoscope. She shifted uncomfortably. The chair groaned just enough to draw their attention. Damn!

Parr looked at her with mild surprise. "It's getting late. Maybe you'd better get going," he muttered to Youngblood. The man left without argument.

Christy stayed put. His eyes studied her, searching her face as if seeing her for the first time.

"I need you to go back into the horoscope and look deeper for information. I need to know how to handle this meeting with the Dragon. Can you do that?"

He talked to her as if she were a co-conspirator. The accuracy of her predictions had garnered his respect. One of her bullets had hit a bull's-eye. She sat a little straighter in the chair. "I haven't looked at planet interaction yet:

squares, conjunctions, opposition, trines. I think I can find what you're looking for."

"Good." His gray eyes were dancing with liquid fire fueled by methamphetamine. It would be hours before his mind stopped racing and allowed his body to rest. Christy knew that if he kept it up, he would be a virtual time bomb set for the ten o'clock meeting with Mondragon.

He motioned her out of the chair and walked her down the hallway. "You're my secret weapon," he whispered, his hot breath stinging her cheek. "You're going to find out what the Colombians are planning for tomorrow."

Christy didn't bother to turn on the light, but stood in the dark as the door was shut and locked. The faint glow from a full moon turned the room translucent. She followed the beams to the window and stared out at the dark outline of grapevines.

"A secret weapon," she murmured aloud. But which target would she shoot for? That was the real secret. She hoped the horoscope had the answers.

All she had were questions.

CHAPTER 29

Christy bent over the desk, staring at the original horoscope she'd done on Parr. The first rays of daylight shone through the window. Only the dogs and sentry were awake. She was exhausted and longed for the oblivion of sleep, but knowing Youngblood was eager to kill her kept her wide awake. Fear won over fatigue.

Events of the night played through her mind, like a CD on repeat mode. Christy believed in fate, but the sudden arrival of Trace Malin was just too much of a coincidence. He was supposed to be locked up in Oregon. The computer said so. Malin was her fool-proof alibi for casting Parr's horoscope—until he showed up at the compound. Why didn't he call her out? Christy wondered. Why did he play along, adding to her story with a few lies of his own?

The appearance of Malin was a heart-stopper, but no match for the terror of hearing Youngblood casually offer to kill her. Hell, the man talked about murdering members of his own gang. She knew her life mattered even less. Parr stood as the only barrier holding Youngblood back. But she could only count on Parr's protection as long as her predictions came true and astrology held his interest.

Her life span was only as long as his attention span.

Tired, weary of the struggle, she gave up, folded her arms on top of the paperwork, and lowered her head. She drifted back to Raisin Ridge Road, the view from her bedroom window, sunlight filtering through the plants, Lennie sprawled on the couch watching a sci-fi show. That life seemed beyond her reach, as though it belonged to somebody else. The past four days, broken down into milliseconds of pain and fear, threatened to eclipse all other memories. She couldn't let that happen.

Sergeant Traynor, Lennie, the deputies—they had to be looking for her. Maybe the first day they'd written her off as AWOL, but she was so stable, so predictable that everyone at the substation would assume she had a good reason for her absence. She hoped, by Thursday, people would be worried. A search party on Friday was too much to wish for—it was payday, and the county frowned on overtime. Besides, there weren't any clues to her kidnaping. The only person who could connect her to

Parr was Wolfe, and he probably didn't even know she was missing.

Did her parents know? She prayed Lennie had the good sense not to contact them. News of her disappearance would send her mother into dramatic high-gear and her give her father a heart attack. They were way too over-protective under normal circumstances.

Of course, Celeste knew. Christy felt her sister's constant presence, sorry for exposing Celeste to this hell. The compound was no place for a nun.

I can handle it, Christy. So can you.

It was a message Christy needed to hear. That's all Celeste could do, offer encouragement and prayers. Going to the authorities was out. When Celeste had visions of the Challenger disaster, every attempt to stop the space shuttle's launch met with ridicule from NASA and censure from the bishop. A psychic nun's word counted for nothing.

Strengthened by the presence of her sister, Christy forced herself to stop speculating on the ripple effect of her abduction and get back to work. In order to hone in astrologically on the next twenty-four hours, she willed her mind to be sharp and set her fears aside.

Opening the ephemeris to the current date, she jotted down the sign and position by degree of the planets Mars, Jupiter, Saturn, Uranus, Neptune, and Pluto in the second circle of the horoscope.

By marking Neptune's current position on the chart, Christy saw that the natal Uranus currently measured a quadrant of ninety degrees, or a four-house square with Neptune. Saturn did the same thing to natal Mars. Benefic Jupiter, she noted, was now in the exact position that malefic Saturn held at Parr's birth. The planets of his past and present, of optimism and pessimism, were in conjunction. Right away, she knew he was in trouble.

She flipped rapidly through the well-thumbed sections of her oldest source book and came to the chapter on planet interaction. It was not as worn as other parts of the manual. Customers were usually satisfied with a general look at the future. Christy saved this section when specific questions and time limits were part of the reading. It was astrological fine-tuning.

The Jupiter-Saturn conjunction, according to the book, was a good time to approach people of power. The Dragon was certainly powerful. But in the same sentence, the book indicated it was a bad time for changes. The messages contradicted each other. Working with the Colombians would put the Black Hearts back on top and put money in their pockets. Ambushing the Dragon would destroy the group if things went wrong. With those kind of odds, why would the planets encourage the meeting at all?

"The Neptune-Uranus square indicates a high level of psychic energy," she read. "Along with increased intuition, Uranus supplies opportunity." Opportunity. That would be the Mondragon's proposal.

But Saturn again turned dour in its square with Mars. It warned that any plans were hazardous. Would danger to Parr translate into danger for herself? The Colombians didn't know who she was, and they might not give a damn that she was being held against her will.

"In addition, this square indicates there are obstacles ahead." One of the obstacles, Christy felt sure, was Parr's drug use. The book noted that this particular planetary alignment "physically drained the person struggling under it while allowing them to stay mentally alert." That sounded like Parr after several days on meth.

She read on. "Under the square of Saturn and Mars, individuals often experience uncontrollable outbursts of temper. An effort must be made to bring plans back into the realm of reality."

It was almost too much. In addition to Youngblood's threats, dangerous Colombians, lethal labs, and bad squares, Christy now had to worry about how much crank Parr snorted. Clean, he might be able to pull off the meeting with Mondragon and come out ahead. Under the influence, Christy knew they would all be at the mercy of Parr's paranoia.

Red warning lights went off in Christy's head when she charted Mars's current course. The planet moved around Parr's chart in a frenzy, squaring off with Jupiter,

Saturn and natal Mars, conjuncting Mercury and the sun. Symbolic of men and war, the aggressiveness of Mars was an element Christy monitored carefully every time she charted. The planet often wreaked havoc and left lives in rubble in the wake of its transit.

Mars's square on Jupiter repeated the warning that this was a time of bad judgement and made Parr the loser in any business deal conducted during this period. Mars squaring Mars also cursed Parr's luck and went on to predict Parr would be boastful and run his mouth in a dangerous way during the upcoming meeting. The warning of the Saturn-Mars square, strengthened by the conjunction of Mars with both Mercury and the sun, gave Christy a good reason to be alarmed. All these planets exerting pressure on Mars could drain Parr, yet the book stressed that his keen perceptions would give him an edge. In another contradictory turn, it also warned that his intuition would be wrong and snap judgements would cause trouble.

One last conjunction remained in the chart: Mars enjoined with Venus. Parr was vulnerable to the influence of a woman. *I'm his Venus,* Christy thought. It was her best, maybe last hope of guiding events to her advantage. All she had to do was pick the right predictions.

Christy pushed the materials away. The stars were sending out mixed signals. She knew the answers were somewhere in the mess—the horoscope seldom failed her—but she also knew that planetary messages could be elusive.

For once, she had no cipher for the code.

Under the influence of the moon, the focus is on mood.

CHAPTER 30

A loud crash and an onslaught of Spanish jerked Christy out of fitful sleep. She raised her head off the desk in confusion. Notes scattered in all directions. Sunlight streamed through the window, and she wondered how long she'd been asleep. The verbal tirade continued, punctuated by the sound of glass breaking in the direction of the kitchen.

"No, you listen to me! You're all a bunch of *penche marranos*. You live in filth and then you bring me here to clean your pigpen! Do I look like a maid?"

Christy listened with her ear pressed against the door. She recognized the agitated voice as Emilina's.

The scuffle came closer until it was right outside the room.

"If I gotta work, she's gotta work. Get her butt out here!"

Trimmer cajoled the woman softly with words Christy couldn't make out. It failed to calm Emilina down.

"No, I'm not cleaning this dump by myself." Emilina pounded on the locked door with her open palm until the hinges rattled. Christy backed away to give her plenty of clearance.

The sound of Parr's voice, quiet, but laced with threat, stopped the commotion. Footsteps retreated down the hall, Emilina leaving cuss words in her wake.

Busy sounds filtered through the walls all afternoon: furniture being moved, laughter, Spanish music from a boom box. Everyone seemed to be pitching in. Christy got a whiff of pine cleaner, and she distinctly heard a vacuum struggling to suck a decade of dirt off the rug.

Spring cleaning in the hottest part of summer. It didn't make sense. Christy slid her hand across her forehead and wiped perspiration from beneath her damp bangs. Nothing in Parr's world made sense. She'd tumbled down the rabbit hole and, like Alice, found all the rules changed. But at least housecleaning was a change for the better.

They must be tidying up for the Colombians. Just like her mother on a cleaning spree when company's coming, Parr wanted to make a good impression. She let out a wry chuckle. Drug dealers with middle-class values. It was the last thing Christy expected to find in Wonderland.

Hours passed and the household settled down. The

piquant smell of chili, cumin, and tortillas wafted down the hallway and tickled Christy's nose. It was the scent of Mexican restaurants: tortilla wedges frying in hot oil, salsa with fresh cilantro, frijoles covered with melted Monterey Jack. She closed her eyes and inhaled deeply. When she opened them, Joey was opening her door.

"Are you hungry? Emilina's cooked us some chow."

He held the door open and she gave him a grateful smile as she walked out.

The kitchen was transformed. Sunshine reflected off gleaming counters. A worn, but clean, tablecloth covered the table. Five places were set with mostly matching silverware.

Emilina, dressed in skin-tight shorts and a tank top cropped to show off her flat stomach, tended a pot of red sauce bubbling on a burner. She turned around, holding a ladle, careful not to drip. "Big difference, huh, *chica*?"

"I'm in shock."

"Yeah, me too." Emilina turned back to the stove. "They conned me into cleaning, but everybody helped. They even bought groceries so I could make them a home-cooked meal. I don't know what got into them."

Neeley and Trimmer strolled into the kitchen, naked from the waist up. Towels were draped around their necks and water dripped off their long hair.

"That pool sure feels good after hauling garbage all day," Neeley said.

"You won't feel so good if you don't stop messing up my clean floor." Emilina punched him hard on the shoulder, and he quickly blotted his hair with the towel. Trimmer grinned and did the same.

This was the flip side of life in the compound, Christy's first glimpse of the good times described by Emilina in their talk a few days earlier. It was obvious the Black Hearts could still band together and get things accomplished, although Christy would stop short of calling them a family. They were a tribe, linked by loyalty and drugs.

Emilina set a basket of warm tortilla chips and bowls of salsa on the table. The men scooped up fistfuls of chips, emptying the basket in record time. She refilled it, the tortilla wedges still glistening with hot oil, and slapped their hands away. "Let somebody else have some."

She piled plates high with enchiladas, Spanish rice, and frijoles, with guacamole on the side. Christy savored the food and appreciated the work that went into the meal. Trimmer and Neeley wolfed the food down.

"Good chow, Emmy." Scraping the last dab of beans with a corn tortilla, Trimmer stood and stretched his lean frame. Christy looked away, uncomfortable with the view. She caught Emilina staring at Trimmer's body in the same hungry way he had eyed her enchiladas.

After Trimmer left to relieve Joey guarding the front,

Emilina fixed a plate and took it to Parr. A few minutes later she returned and slammed the stoneware on the table.

"He says he don't want it. I went to all this work, and he won't eat."

Neeley, steadily shoveling rice and beans in his mouth, paused and tried to swallow. "He's cranking up again. Here, give me his food. Shame to let it go to waste."

Christy's stomach churned. It had nothing to do with the spicy food and everything to do with Neeley's statement.

"I have to see Parr."

"Eat. He's not going nowhere." Emilina had a point.

Christy reluctantly pushed her unfinished dinner away, knowing it would be gone when she returned. She stood up. "I have to see him now, before he does any more damage. He needs to know his future."

❦

Parr was in the dark.

Christy entered the living room and saw him sitting in the recliner, lit only by a sliver of light coming through a gap in the curtains. The room had been aired out and the clutter removed. It felt a lot cleaner and more spacious.

Without warning, the table lamp snapped on. Parr's eyes were red and his pupils enlarged. It was a sight Christy expected, but not what she wanted to see.

"I hope you got some good news for me." His hands held the lacquer box containing the crank, and his fingers fiddled with the catch. He cocked his head toward the empty chair in the corner, but this time Christy chose the footstool.

She didn't look him in the face, but glared at the box. "You have to stop using."

"Nobody tells me what to do, bitch."

"You're going to need a clear head when you meet the Dragon."

Parr studied her face under the fringe of bangs. "Is this you talkin' or the horoscope?"

"The horoscope."

Slowly, his hand moved away from the clasp. He placed the box carefully on the table. "All right. No more until the meet is over."

Could she trust him? "What about the drugs you've already taken?"

He rubbed his eyes and his hand continued upward until it swept the hair back from his face. He looked exhausted. "How clean do I need to be?"

"Spotless."

He shrugged. "Maybe Emilina's got some downers in her purse. Something to level me off."

Drugs to counteract drugs. It sounded dangerous and downright self-defeating. But then, her first-hand knowledge of pharmaceuticals was limited to aspirin and cold medicine.

"Maybe you should eat something. Emilina made a terrific meal."

"I'd have to smoke a couple joints to work up my appetite."

Another bad compromise. Parr, no doubt, understood his body chemistry, but he seemed like a toxic waste dump to Christy.

"Don't worry, I'll be clean by tonight. Now, what do the stars say? Should we work with the Colombians or not?"

"There's a lot of activity centered around Mars and involving the major planets. I'm interpreting it as a sign that you should meet with the Dragon. It looks like a great opportunity. Your life is going to change because of contact with this man."

Parr sank back in the lounger. "That's good to hear. I've been waiting a long time for this shot. It's comin' together, just like you said it would." He glanced at Christy and caught her biting her lower lip. "What? You're holding back something."

"There's danger." She searched Parr's face. "You have to stay calm around the Colombian. Watch your temper, pick your words carefully. Your intuition's very strong right now, but the drugs might diminish your perceptions. You can't be paranoid."

That's all she could tell Parr without putting herself in danger. She'd told him what he wanted to hear. And it was the truth, more or less. She even sprinkled in a few more predictions to convince him it was the entire reading. Still, she avoided his penetrating gaze, afraid he might read her mind and know there was more.

"You're worried about me, aren't you?"

Of course, she was worried. Her life depended on this drug-crazed, paranoid megalomaniac. One wrong signal and she'd find herself in the crossfire, a hare in a pack of dogs. "Yes, I'm worried."

He leaned forward and reached out to her, touching her lightly on the wrist. It took all her willpower not to recoil.

"Fate brought us together—fate and Trace Malin." His fingers, deathly cold, caressed her hand. "You did real good, you got me back on track. If this meet works out with the Colombians, I'm gonna let you go. That's a promise." He leaned back in his chair. "'Course, Blood's gonna be a problem. He wants to waste you because he's scared you'll snitch us off."

He said it so casually. Christy realized that as long as he stayed drug-free, she had a chance to get out of this mess alive. The next time he crashed off the meth, Blood would have the chance he waited for.

Blood didn't strike her as a patient man.

"How could I snitch? I don't know anything." With freedom a promise away, Christy found it easy to grovel. "I don't even know where I'm at, I couldn't lead anybody back here. It's only been three days. You could let me go right now and it would be like this never happened."

But Parr wasn't paying attention to her. His eyes were focused over her head. She turned and saw a shadowy form leaning against the doorjamb.

"How long have you been standing there, Emmy?"

"Long enough." She turned on her heel and left.

CHAPTER 31

It was 7:15 p.m., only forty-five minutes until the meet, when things began to go wrong. Parr wanted Emilina out of the compound, but the Cadillac wouldn't budge. There was no time for Neeley to tinker with the engine. Parr needed him as muscle, not as a mechanic. As a result, Christy found herself sequestered in the bedroom with an extremely pissed off Emilina.

The enraged woman paced the room, and Christy watched with the trepidation of a cat penned in with a pit bull. Every so often, Emilina hurled an epithet in Spanish at her. Christy only caught a few slang words, but was fairly certain her mother's honor and her own legitimacy were under attack. Which was okay, as long as things didn't get physical.

Up to now, Emilina had been an wary ally, or, at the very least, a hostage sympathizer. But something changed after dinner. Christy had a feeling the anger was ignited at the sight of Parr touching her hand. Possessiveness, she could understand, but Emilina had nothing to be jealous about. As soon as the woman calmed down, Christy would set her straight.

The pacing stopped. Emilina turned and faced Christy, her hands resting on her hips like a gunslinger ready to draw down.

"Okay, puta, what the hell's goin' on? How come I'm stuck in here with you? Somethin' big's happening. I think you know what it is."

Parr had locked his former mistress completely out of the game plan. This was news to Christy. Why was he keeping the Colombian's visit under wraps? Emilina saw drug dealers come and go at the compound all the time. Why the sudden lack of trust?

Emilina went to her handbag and took out a pack of cigarettes. "Yeah, you know," she muttered, fumbling with a lighter. "I see the way he looks at you. I see you two holding hands. He gets me to cook and clean, but now he's tellin' you his secrets."

"You've got it all wrong—"

"No, you got it wrong. He's cleaned up for you. He used to do that for me. It ain't gonna last. You don't mean shit to him."

Getting Emilina back on her side was more important than keeping Parr's confidence. Besides, she had no loyalties to these lowlifes. She wasn't a member of the Black Hearts, she was their prisoner. No rules applied.

"Okay, I'll tell you what I heard. Do you know Trace Malin?"

Emilina narrowed her eyes. "Sure. Trace." She tilted her chin up. "Me and him had a thing going before he went north. He's gonna look me up when he gets out of prison."

"He's out. He's coming here tonight. And he's bringing a friend with him, a Colombian drug dealer by the name of Mondragon."

That caught Emilina off guard. "The Dragon? The Dragon's coming here? Tonight?"

"Any time now. I guess that's why they cleaned the house." She finally had Emilina's attention. "Listen, it's not what you think between Lloyd and me. There's absolutely nothing going on behind your back."

But Emilina wasn't listening. All of her features softened and she radiated an inner glow that gave her cheeks a natural blush and erased ten years from her face. Christy wondered what kind of drugs she was on.

"The Dragon. Here, in this house. How the hell did Lloyd do it?" She looked at Christy. "You don't know who's coming here tonight, do you? This ain't another nickel-and-dime-bag street dealer. This man's a legend. All over the barrio, they talk about 'El Dragon.' He helps his people, kinda like Robin Hood. But the Dragon don't steal from rich people, he gives cocaine to the poor to sell to the rich. He gets a cut, and everybody makes money."

Christy could see, by Emilina's avaricious expression, that the woman's mind saw dollar signs like a cash register. "Men with money are always handsome," she informed Christy, as if it were written on a Lincoln penny. "Bet on it."

She headed toward the bathroom, handbag in tow. "I've got to get ready," she announced, flopping the bag on the counter. She unzipped the purse and out tumbled lipsticks, foundation, a powder compact, hairspray, a set of travel curlers, blush, mascara, fingernail polish, and a palette containing twenty-eight shades of eyeshadow.

Christy watched Emilina spackle new make-up over the old. "I could be wrong, but I don't think we're invited to the meeting."

Holding the mascara wand like a weapon, Emilina turned. "Whatcha talkin' about? They damn well better let me meet this guy."

Christy shrugged. "The door's locked. I think they plan to keep it that way until Mondragon leaves."

"That door's locked to keep you from gettin' out. Not me. They know they're in big trouble if they lock me in." She turned her attention back to the mirror.

Emilina's stubbornness irritated Christy. "We're both in this room and the door's locked. I'd say they plan on keeping us here. Both of us."

Emilina threw a powder compact across the room. The plastic case shattered as it hit the wall. Her glossed mouth twisted into an ugly sneer. "Not me, bitch!"

They both heard the car pull into the driveway at the same time. The dogs barked and a car door slammed. Emilina swept the cosmetics off the counter and into the open bag. She took one final look in the bathroom mirror, licked her index finger to smooth an eyebrow, smiled at her reflection, and snapped off the light.

"I'm ready to meet the Dragon," she announced.

She walked over to the window, released the lock, and pushed hard until the glass slid down the track.

All hell broke loose.

∽∾∽

Parr and his men couldn't get the door open fast enough. Christy hunkered down in the chair and listened as they fumbled at the lock while the alarm wailed on and on. Finally, Trimmer rushed in, pushed Emilina aside, and shut the window. The mechanical screams stopped. They all stared at one another in the silence.

"What the hell do you think you're doing?"

Youngblood blocked the doorway. His chest heaved and his eyes bulged. He looked like a man on the verge of a heart attack.

"I wanted some air in this room. Guess I forgot about

the alarm." She stared him down, daring him to call her a liar.

Youngblood looked capable of committing double homicide as his last act on earth. He started toward Emilina, but she held up her bag as a shield. Christy hoped she had a weapon buried in the make-up.

"Hey, Emilina! Get over here, girl, and let me look at you."

Trace's voice broke the tension. He towered over the others and held out his arms. Emilina brushed past Youngblood and into the protection of Trace's embrace.

"Trace, you got an earring," she teased. "And your hair's real long again. Ugh, you gotta let me dye it. Where'd you get all that gray?"

"Behind bars, you little jumpin' bean. Are you the one settin' off the alarm back here? You about scared me and my buddy to death. I was flashing back to a prison break."

"You got a friend from prison with you, Trace?"

"No, honey, I wouldn't bring any ex-cons home for a visit. Too many bad influences around here already. But I bet my buddy would just love to meet you and your girl-friend."

"She's not my girlfriend," Emilina sneered, but it was too late.

Trace extended his hand and pulled Christy out of the chair.

Reluctantly, Christy followed the others down the hall, propelled by Trace's hand on her shoulder. Unlike Emilina, she wasn't in any hurry to meet the legendary Colombian. She'd feel safer locked away in the room, out of everybody's way. If only Emilina had kept her hands off the damn window! Now, like it or not, she was going to hear all the details of the meet between Parr and the Dragon.

Parr promised to let her go. Would he mean it after her head was filled with incriminating info? Would Youngblood let her walk free and clear?

Christy knew everything said in the meet brought her that much closer to a death sentence.

It was a long walk to the living room.

CHAPTER 32

She felt Mondragon's presence as soon as she entered the living room. Parr sat in his usual spot, but the chair on the other side of the lamp was occupied. The man leaned back, his face in shadows. A gold pinky ring caught the light. The writhing shape of a dragon with ruby eyes caught Emilina's eye. She stepped forward, stealing the spotlight.

With the tiniest flick of her head to make her glistening curls dance, she said, "Why don't you introduce us, Lloyd?"

He glared a warning at the woman. "You've caused enough trouble tonight. Sit your ass down."

The visitor stood up in one smooth motion and emerged from the shadows. He took Emilina's hand as if it were fine bone china. Christy wondered if he was going to kiss it, but he gave it a gesture somewhere between a handshake and a caress.

"Luis Rojas Mondragon," he said in a voice tinged with an accent and at the level of a low purr.

Glowing at his touch and blushing through layers of make-up, Emilina stood rooted to the rug. Mondragon leaned to his left and looked around her at Christy.

"And you are…"

Christy couldn't say her name. Was she supposed to reveal her identity to a stranger? She looked helplessly at Parr for direction.

"That's my astrologer."

"Ah." Mondragon accepted this answer as though astrologers were commonplace among drug dealers.

Unwilling to share the Dragon's attention, Emilina said, "I've heard stories about you." She launched into a litany of all the stories from the barrio. Mondragon looked surprised. And uncomfortable.

Parr gave a signal. Trimmer took firm hold of Emilina's shoulders and pulled her back toward the couch. Christy followed and sat as far away as possible from the action.

From a safe distance, her eyes lingered over the stranger, starved for a visual change from the scruffy members of Parr's gang. Mondragon was a feast. His thick hair, Indian-straight with just the slightest wave above his forehead, shone like onyx in the lamplight. A dark, well-trimmed moustache ended precisely at the corners of his mouth. His lips were full and sensuous, like a starlet with collagen injections.

"You're a hell of a lot younger than I figured on," Parr said.

Mondragon nodded but offered no explanation. He looked young to Christy, too, maybe twenty-eight. Much too young to bear the weight of his reputation. Maybe cartel children were trained from infancy in the fine art of drug dealing.

Even if Emilina had not mentioned his wealth, Christy would still have known he was upper crust. His clothes were understated: levis worn to the suppleness of fine suede; exotic reptile skin reincarnated as boots; and a simple, well-cut shirt, open at the neck and probably sporting a designer label Christy wouldn't recognize. It was in a shade of cream her mother called "ecru," and it picked up the caramel tones of his skin as if created for that very purpose.

"You speak English pretty good for a foreigner." Parr looked at the Colombian with contempt as he poured a Corona into a clean beer glass and produced a perfect head of foam. He offered it to his guest.

"I studied at UCLA. I majored in business."

The amenities out of the way, Parr, his cooker, and the Colombian began bargaining. How much ephedrine, the delivery date, when they would do the cook, how to divide the product for sales. Parr assured the Dragon that they had a safe place to process the meth, an old barn on property under his control. They had successfully cooked there in the past without attracting the attention of the authorities. In fact, Parr boasted, hush money and death threats kept the farmer who owned the land looking the other way.

Huddled in the corner, Christy found herself mesmerized by the scene unfolding before her. It was business as usual and not that much different from other business ventures. Except these were drug dealers, and the final result of their transaction would be a felony.

She watched Parr's performance with relief. His drug-induced paranoia had disappeared, and he appeared calm and decisive. Her coaching, and the horoscope, were both paying off.

"We're gonna need to see a sample of this ephedrine you got, test the quality," Blood said.

Mondragon glanced coolly from Youngblood to Parr, as if to ask, "Who's in charge here?" Then he shrugged and motioned for Trace to open a small gym bag. Trace retrieved a bundle wrapped in butcher paper and sealed with tape. "Please," the Dragon said softly to Youngblood, "Take the package. Test it. I think you'll find it satisfactory."

Christy floated on the cadence of his voice. She imagined it was the tone of upper class Colombians. To her ear, every word, every vowel was a sonata.

The discussion continued among the men, but Christy wasn't listening.

She was watching the Dragon's eyes There was no hardness in them, no glint of ruthlessness meant to intimidate his enemies. Somehow, this made him seem even more dangerous.

Parr watched her.

He suddenly turned to Mondragon. "You got any ID on you?"

The question hung in the air like the slap of a dueling glove. Mondragon didn't react, but his refusal to answer spoke volumes.

"I want her to do your horoscope," Parr said, pointing at Christy. "You got a problem with that?"

"This ain't the time for your bullshit, Lloyd," Youngblood warned between clenched teeth. "We're doin' business here."

But Mondragon pulled his wallet out of his pants pocket. He motioned to Christy with a manicured finger.

Her legs trembled as she walked across the room. She felt the Dragon's presence, like a magnet, pulling her toward him. Self-consciousness flooded over her—a week's worth of dirt on her clothes, stringy hair, glasses hanging at an odd angle across her face. Her face felt bare and exposed. She wished she had put on a little of Emilina's makeup before facing this man at close range.

Emilina gave her a searing look as she hurried past. Danger signals flashed in her eyes. Trace moved his arm to pin Emilina to the couch.

Mondragon held an Oregon driver's license out for her inspection. Christy bent forward and squinted at the birthdate. He was a Sagittarian, and he wore Obsession.

"I believe in astrology," Mondragon said to Christy. "In my country, astrologers are highly respected. We consult them just as we consult doctors, stock brokers, or priests. But few men are lucky enough to have a private astrologer."

"She's on loan," Youngblood muttered.

Parr shot him a damning look.

"Please, cast my horoscope. Your trust is important to me."

Christy looked deep into the velvet brown of his eyes. Was that last statement meant for her or Parr?

"We need a day to pick up equipment and haul it out to the barn."

Parr's voice broke the spell. Christy took a few awkward steps back.

"Tomorrow's good, there's not much traffic on Sundays. The cops are scarce too. Do you think you can start the cook by Monday, Blood?"

"If the ephedrine passes the test."

"And if I like what she sees in the horoscope," Parr added.

Youngblood rolled his eyes and balled his fists.

Parr ignored him.

Mondragon got up to leave. He went up to Christy and lightly touched her shoulder. "I hope you find what you're looking for in my chart," he said quietly.

She watched as he left the room. He seemed to take all the light with him.

As soon as the door closed, Trace released his hold on Emilina, and she bolted from the couch.

"You bitch!" Emilina's venom was strong. "Don't think I don't know your game. First, you flirt with Parr so now he thinks he needs you. Then you try to make Trimmer and Joey promise to help you. Now, you weave your spell on the Dragon, and he doesn't even look at me."

The fingernails came out of nowhere. They whipped across Christy's cheek like the poisonous sting of the scorpion.

Trimmer pushed Emilina aside and hurried Christy out of range of the woman's fury, but not her curses.

"I wish you'd never come here. Now I'm gonna make sure you don't leave alive."

Neptune is a test of faith and morality.

CHAPTER 33

The throbbing of her cheek woke Christy. Sometime during the night she had rolled on her side and pressed her face into the soiled towel she used as a pillow. The coarse fabric bit into the scratches from last night's confrontation with Emilina. Christy got up, went into the bathroom, and ran cold water over the sour washcloth. She dabbed at the dried blood on her face.

What was Emilina's problem? Christy inspected the razor-thin marks across her cheek. The cuts were superficial, but not Emilina's motive. The sharp fingernails were a warning to back off from the Black Heart men. And the Dragon.

His touch had shocked Christy. The thought disgusted her. Although the physical relationship between Parr and Emilina died years ago, her actions signaled jealousy.

And her possessiveness extended to Trimmer. The sexual tension between those two was hotter than Emilina's salsa.

But Christy knew, standing there in the tiny bathroom, that the problem wasn't Emilina's claim on Parr or Trimmer. The real complication was Luis Mondragon.

Christy's face suddenly felt hot from more than just the scratches. She looked at her reflection in the mirror: filthy hair, grimy clothes, circles under her eyes. Okay, so he was attractive. But there was no flirting going on.

The entire scene with Mondragon played over in her mind, this time from Emilina's vantage point. She saw herself walk across the room toward the Dragon, lean in too close to look at the driver's license, hold contact with his eyes a little longer than was wise. She was drawn to the man with such intensity that she ignored the danger around her.

So, that's what set Emilina off. Christy moved the tepid washcloth from her cheek to her forehead where a tension headache was erupting. Emilina thought she was competing for Mondragon's attention. Christy ran her finger down her cheek. The scratches were light penance.

Back in the bedroom, Christy sat in the corner on the floor, closed her eyes, and leaned her head back against the wall. The damp rag dropped into her lap. Is that what Parr thought as well? Parr's eyes were sharp when he wasn't on drugs, and they were like a hawk's last night.

She knew the exact moment she felt fear from his scrutiny.

The image of Luis Mondragon broke through the pain at her temples. The Colombian was handsome, she had to admit. The fluid movements, his composure, the concern in his eyes, the muscles lightly defined by his shirt, the tapering waist—

"But he's a drug dealer," Christy moaned.

There was no way she could be attracted to him. She worked for the sheriff, and this man was the antithesis of everything she believed in. Law and order. Right and wrong. Good and evil. This man brought the drugs that were sold to children and hooked their parents. He earned his living destroying the lives of others.

Yet, he looked as though none of the dirt touched him. The Dragon appeared like the mythical knight in Armani armor. Every cell in her body screamed out, "Save me!" But why should one drug dealer make her feel safe from the others? Where did he get this power?

She hugged her knees and rested her forehead on her kneecaps. Images of Patty Hearst ran through her mind. There was a word for it: the Stockholm Syndrome. Was she identifying with her captors? She'd been with the Black Hearts five days now. Every hour she felt herself being dragged deeper into the swirling currents of their world. Were the lines beginning to blur? Could she really be getting the hots for a Colombian drug lord?

What would her mother think? He certainly wasn't son-in-law material.

The headache wasn't going anywhere, and it would turn into a migraine if she continued along this train of thought. She glared at the astrology books on the table. Migraine or no migraine, Parr expect Mondragon's horoscope from her.

His chart would hold some answers. The throbbing at her temples eased as she felt a surge of anticipation. Christy went to the table and pulled out a piece of paper. She sat down and drew a circle then intersected it with six lines. She looked up his birthdate and quickly filled in the planetary symbols in the proper spots.

His chart was well-balanced, although the ninth house had the heaviest activity. He was a traveler, which was obvious from his drug activities and the fact that he was so far from home. Uranus and Pluto indicated opportunity as impetus for his travels and violence as a result. Often, according to the interpretation in the book, he brought order out of chaos, but not without force.

Mars, his most masculine sign, was also in the ninth house under the sign of Virgo. Although most Sagittarian men were womanizers, Virgo made the Dragon very slow to get involved with a woman, almost shy. This surprised Christy. Perhaps it was the nature of his job and the fact that he was on the move that kept him from marriage. The Virgo Mars also made him very logical in his approach to love and analytical about relationships.

Intrigued, Christy looked at his Venus. Located in the sign of Scorpio, this planet made him intense and passionate with the right woman. He didn't take romance lightly, Christy mused as she massaged her eyelids.

In the fifth house, Mondragon had the planet Jupiter under the sign of Taurus. Amazingly enough, he was everything she'd want in a husband: domestic, reliable, patient, and offering security along with his love.

Security didn't include a home, apparently. The man had a hard time committing to a place to live, and he was moody about setting down permanent roots. On the other hand, he had a healthy relationship with his parents and relatives. He also had a lot of responsibility in the family at a young age, according to the chart.

Information about the Dragon's sexuality, husband potential, or how well he was regarded by his family would not interest Lloyd Parr. Christy scouted the circle to find something that would.

Mercury in the first house under Capricorn showed Mondragon to have leadership qualities. He was a conservative, persevering, and gentle man who, nevertheless, ran an international drug operation. His intuition was apparently as high as Parr's, and not as likely to be impaired by narcotics. Neptune in the sign of Scorpio made him a dangerous enemy and a loner, secretive and cold-blooded.

Still, Parr's sixth sense might tell him the same things the horoscope revealed. She flipped to the current date and charted the second circle to see what Mondragon's life looked like right now.

Other than Uranus and Neptune transiting into the second house, which confirmed a major money increase—probably profits from the upcoming lab—there was little in Mondragon's current chart that would interest Parr.

She had to come up with something, a key bit of information that would make Parr feel he had an edge on the Colombian. Since it wasn't apparent in the horoscope, her only option was to create a new chart, one with an obvious vulnerability, an Achilles heel. Give Parr a target to shoot at, Christy decided. Having made up her mind to cheat, the headache loosened its grip.

At that moment, the key turned in the lock. Breakfast. The charting made her famished. She looked up, expecting Trimmer or Neeley. The papers in her hands fell to the floor.

It was Youngblood.

He held a pair of handcuffs.

CHAPTER 34

The handcuffs bit into her wrists when Christy struggled, so she kept her arms slack as they led her toward Youngblood's pickup. The man's massive hand held her upper arm in a grip as tight as the cuffs. She knew it was useless to struggle. Trimmer held her other arm loosely above the elbow.

"Get in back," Youngblood ordered Neeley and Joey. They mounted the bumper and vaulted into the bed of the truck. Youngblood jerked open the passenger door of the cab and climbed in, pulling Christy after him as he shifted his bulk into the driver's seat. Trimmer settled next to her and pulled out a semi-automatic. He trained it on Christy.

"We'll take the backroad out," Youngblood announced, shifting the truck into gear.

"Why? Do you think the compound is being watched?" Trimmer asked.

"If you kept your eyes open, you'd notice strangers hangin' around down the road from the house," Blood snapped.

"Raisin pickers, that's all. They come this time every year."

"Maybe. Maybe not. It don't hurt to take precautions."

The truck hurtled through the grapevines following a path carved out by tractor treads. With every bump and jolt, Christy glanced at the gun pointed at her. Trimmer's finger wasn't firm on the trigger, but still she worried that it might go off.

Christy knew she had a slim chance of escaping whatever fate Youngblood had in mind, but she stubbornly clung to hope. Maybe Highway Patrol would pull the truck over since there was a law against passengers riding in the bed. Or maybe the house was under surveillance and deputies had roadblocks set up where the dirt path joined paved road. Her mind worked feverishly on the maybes to block out the inevitables.

The pickup pulled out to the main road. It was devoid of familiar green and white sheriff's patrol cars. Christy's hopes waned as Youngblood pressed hard on the gas pedal, careful to exceed the speed limit only as much as country driving allowed.

The truck approached a white church on the driver's side. Trimmer roughly pushed her shoulder down until the top of her head barely peeked over the dashboard. The handcuffs pressed hard into her back. Christy could hear voices calling out and car engines starting as people spilled out from Sunday services. She struggled to sit up but Trimmer's strong hand held her down. The truck slowed to a crawl as it edged past the crowd. Looking up, the only thing Christy could see from her slouching position was a church steeple, a single spire flanked by four smaller spires on each side.

Once past the church, they let her sit up. The truck picked up speed, and Youngblood made a touch-and-go stop at a four-way intersection. Just past the stop, on the right, stood a small cemetery. Bright flowers dotted the graveyard and Mylar balloons danced lazily in the hot morning air. A family gathered around a group of headstones and a woman knelt to place flowers on a grave. Christy, recoiling from the sight of tombstones, turned her face away and stared blankly ahead.

They followed the road for another ten minutes, then Youngblood braked sharply for a stop sign and made an abrupt right turn. The narrow road was pocked with potholes. The pickup scattered crows feasting off road kill. Only a few ranch houses broke up the miles of grapevines and orchards. The truck flew past the scenery, unchallenged by another vehicle.

The truck slowed and Christy knew they were nearing their destination. She looked around, but all she saw were vineyards. Youngblood eased the truck alongside a barely visible opening in the rows of grapes. Looking in every direction to assure himself there were no witnesses, he turned onto the path, and the truck was swallowed up by dense foliage.

It wasn't long before the coiling grapevines gave way to an open field. Rusted barbed wire and a "No Trespassing" sign warned away unwelcome visitors. A barn, weathered gray and sagging in the eaves, had doors bolted with a new brass lock that brightly reflected the sun. Neeley jumped out of the back and swung the gate wide to allow the truck to enter.

Trimmer glanced over at the barn then at Christy. "Does Parr know about this?"

"He told me last night to get things in order. I gotta check the equipment for the cook."

Youngblood dragged Christy out of the cab of the truck. Her wrists throbbed and she bit hard on the inside of her lip to keep from crying out.

Everyone stood in a semi-circle, self-consciously looking at her and then at each other. Nobody dared to look Youngblood directly in the eye.

Trimmer broke the silence. "I don't think it's a good idea to let her see where we cook."

"Yeah, Parr told us he didn't want her out of the

compound." Neeley looked to Trimmer and Joey for support. They bobbed their heads in agreement.

Youngblood glared at them. His mouth contorted as if he'd just tasted something disgusting and he spat on the ground.

He looked in the direction of a dry irrigation ditch. "I think she needs to get her head out of the stars and get a look at the real world."

Trimmer blanched. "No, Blood, you're going too far. Let's get her in the truck and head back to the compound."

"The hell with you." Youngblood grabbed Christy's upper arm and pulled her, half stumbling, half trotting, to the scrub oak at the edge of the canal bank with a trickle of water flowing at the bottom.

At first, Christy couldn't tell what it was. It was shoved into the crevice of a tree root that had grown through the dirt wall of the canal. Just a pile of rags with something shriveled and leathery balanced on top.

Then Christy saw a running shoe, ripped and caked with dirt. Attached to it was the remains of an ankle. Her eyes went out of focus for a second. Then she took a harder look again at the ball on top of the rags. It was a head, the eyes gone, the nose partially destroyed. Hair trailed through the remains like dry grass.

"Meet Johnny Blue," Youngblood said.

Christy bent over and retched in the weeds. She

could hear Youngblood's laughter ringing above her head.

"I thought the body would be gone by now," Joey said uneasily.

"Naw, we screwed up," Neeley replied. "We were off by a month on the water schedule."

The men stared at the corpse cradled in the tree root while Christy's dry heaves subsided. She wanted to faint, but her trembling body stubbornly held on to consciousness. Only the steel-like grip of Youngblood's hand kept her on her feet.

"Now the bitch knows everything," Youngblood said to the group. "It's Lloyd's fault. He never shoulda let her sit in on the meet. I mean to put a stop to this bullshit." He looked at Trimmer. "Go get my kit from the truck."

Trimmer fetched a small case from a hidden compartment under the driver's seat. It was leather, embossed with a black heart.

"There's enough in there for a hot shot. Get it ready."

Trimmer stared down at the kit then into Christy's frightened face. He shook his head. "I can't do it, Blood."

Youngblood narrowed his eyes. "Why not? You did it for Johnny Blue. Or did you suddenly forget how to fix?"

"I just can't. Not this time." Trimmer tried to hand him the kit, but Youngblood waved it away. "Neeley. Take the kit."

Neeley took the case and opened it. He removed a spoon with a handle which curved back to the bowl, and a lighter embossed with a black heart. He also retrieved two bindles of black tar heroin and a vial of water and set to work.

Trimmer watched with agitation. "Blood, are you crazy? What happens when Lloyd finds out?"

"I'll tell him the bitch escaped. When they open up the irrigation gates, she'll be floating up the canal and out of his life. Anyway, he's so wrapped up with this Columbian deal, he'll forget all about her in a couple days." Youngblood looked around the group. "Every man here better back up my story."

The heroin had turned to liquid. Neeley picked up a cigarette filter from the kit and dipped it into the bowl of the spoon. It soaked up the drug like a sponge. He inserted the needle into the filter and drew the plunger back. The syringe filled with the deadly dose. Tapping the tip lightly against the metal, Neeley held it out to Youngblood.

The needle looked massive to Christy. She squirmed and pulled away from the instrument. Youngblood's hand gripped her arm like a vise. The pain of the handcuffs cutting into her wrists did not even register.

"Go ahead," Youngblood urged Neeley.

Neeley looked around him in confusion. "Me?"

"Go ahead!" Youngblood commanded.

But Neeley stepped back and shook his head in quick, jerking motions. "Un-uh. I can't do this. I promised."

"What the hell are you talking about?"

"She kept her mouth shut and didn't tell Lloyd what she saw in the horoscope about me. I promised I wouldn't hurt her. I gave my word."

Youngblood glared at him then snatched the needle out of his hand. "Your word don't mean shit." He turned to his son. "Okay, Joey, this is your chance to lose your cherry." He held the needle out to the boy.

"I can't, Dad."

Youngblood lost his patience. "I'm giving you a chance to stop being a pussy, boy. One shot and it's over. She won't feel a thing."

Joey's eyes welled up with tears. "I can't do it. I'll do most anything else you want, but I can't kill her, Dad."

They felt Youngblood's rage like the waves of heat rising off the ground. "You ain't any son of mine unless you're man enough to kill." He breathed deep and waited for his son to take the syringe. "You disgust me," he finally said in a deadly quiet voice. "You don't have the brains to be a cooker or the balls to be a killer." He turned away from the boy, who looked as though the needle had plunged into his heart.

Christy was numb. Youngblood's hold on her arm

had tightened as he spilled his venom on his son. The men had kept their word and refused to hurt her. But there was no escape from Youngblood.

As she listened to Youngblood bully the others, her spirit gave up quietly. Tired of the pain, tired of the fear, she stopped resisting. Thoughts of her parents, Celeste, and Grandma Good entered her mind. No one close to her had ever died. How ironic that the first death she'd have to deal with would be her own. She realized she'd been sleepwalking through life, shying away from its pleasures and possibilities. It was almost like being dead.

Now, her senses came to life. She could smell the dry grass, feel the hot hint of a breeze, taste the Valley dust. It was as though the Earth demanded she take a last look.

She turned her head away from Youngblood and let the sun beat full on her face. Beyond the canal flowed endless rows of grapevines. The view ended with a stand of palms, seven of them in a row. One palm towered over the rest. They watched from a distance, like sentinels standing guard.

Christy closed her eyes to seal the image in her mind and said a prayer of two words:

Remember this.

CHAPTER 35

Christy braced for the sharp stab of the needle. A new sound filled the background and the whine of an engine broke through her numbness.

She opened her eyes just as the Cadillac plunged through the open gate and did a half-turn skid before coming to a stop in front of the barn. Parr bolted from the driver's seat. Emilina emerged more slowly from the passenger side. Her lip was split and bleeding. One eye was half-closed and turning purple.

"Put down the needle, Blood," Parr ordered.

Youngblood held the syringe steady in one hand. Christy felt a yank and suddenly she found herself positioned between Blood and Parr.

"I'm doing this for your own good, Lloyd."

Parr reached behind his back and pulled a semi-automatic from his waistband. "And I'm doin' this for my own good, Blood. Let her go or I swear I'll kill you."

"You don't have a clean shot, Lloyd. One way or the other, she dies."

Youngblood laughed. He let go of her arm. For a split second Christy felt free of his grip. Then she let out a scream as he grabbed the cuffs and twisted them. Her arms were taut behind her, veins waiting.

Youngblood drove the needle toward Christy's arm.

The gunshot was muffled. Youngblood wavered. The needle slipped through his fingers and landed by Christy's foot. He sank to his knees, still gripping the handcuffs and pulling Christy down with him until Trimmer pulled her out of his grasp.

Christy was amazed at Parr's marksmanship—she'd never heard the bullet go by. But Parr held the gun in ready position as he stared past her, an expression of surprise on his face. Reluctantly, she turned to look.

Youngblood wavered on his knees. Joey stood behind him, confused and tearful. The weapon in the boy's hand shook uncontrollably. His T-shirt was splattered dark red from the close range of the target. He made a move toward his father and caught the body as it slumped to the ground.

"Hell, Joey. What'd ya go and shoot him in the back for?" Parr lowered his weapon and slipped it back into his waistband. "Now all I got is another corpse and no cooker."

სოცი

It was a tense ride back to the compound. Christy sat in the backseat of the convertible between Joey and Emilina while Parr, looking pasty in the sunlight, drove. Neeley and Trimmer were left behind to dispose of Youngblood. She saw them rolling his body toward the canal just before she was shoved into the car.

"My dad oughta be buried proper," Joey muttered from his corner of the car. He had his gun out, as instructed by Parr, but showed little interest in guarding her.

"You shoulda thought about that before you killed him," Parr pointed out. "The canal's as good a grave as any. By tomorrow, they'll have the water running and he'll float all the way to the next county. Your dad always liked to tube down the river with a six pack of beer in the summer."

"You better hope they turn on the water this time." Emilina's words were slurred from the swelling of her lip.

"I double-checked the water schedule myself. It's gonna go as planned. `Course—" Parr glanced in the rear view mirror at Joey. "—I never figured on two bodies. Blue's gonna fall apart as soon as the water hits him, but Blood'll be a floater. Hope nobody spots him."

"They'll figure it's a swimming accident," Emilina said.

"Accidents don't come with bullet holes," Parr shot back. His eyes flashed angrily into the rear view mirror. "I blame you, too, Emilina. Blood would be alive if you'd told me his plan up front. You made me waste too much time beating it outta you."

His eyes then shifted to Joey. "You can't stay at the compound anymore, boy. You're gonna have to stay with your ma. Play stupid if the cops come nosing around askin' questions."

"What am I gonna tell my mom?"

Parr's face flushed with anger. "I got a bigger problem. What the hell am I gonna tell the Colombians tomorrow when they come ready to do the cook? 'Sorry, but my cooker just got blown away by his boy. Nice doing business with ya.'" Parr shook his head. "You really screwed me on this."

Joey's mouth gaped open. "Me? You woulda killed him if you'd had a good shot!"

"But I didn't. Hell, I was just givin' your dad a warning. Do you think I'd shoot a man I've partnered with for twenty years to save this bitch? That her life means more than a deal that'll bring in money and keep me in crank? Naw, that wasn't in your head when you shot your old man." Parr adjusted the rear view so the Joey could see his penetrating stare. "Blood was rough on you, boy. He beat you and called you a pussy, gave you nothing worth shit when you were growing up. I know you wanted to kill him, that's just natural. I wanted to murder my dad, but he saved me the trouble by dying of cancer. I'm just saying your timing coulda been better, that's all. You put me in a bind, boy."

Christy listened to Parr lay blame on the boy, not surprised or even appalled at the way he twisted everything to suit his conscience. Death was an inconvenience to him, nothing more. She glanced over at Joey. His face showed his struggle to deal with the horror of his actions. She wanted to thank him for saving her life, but knew it would trespass on his grief.

They rode in silence. The scenery flew by as Parr ignored speed limits and backroads, taking the main route in his rush to get home. As they neared the compound, he ordered Christy to get down on the floor of the car.

"See those two wetbacks parked on the side of the road?" she heard Parr tell Joey. "That Chevy was there when I left this morning."

But Joey was not interested. "Maybe they're waitin' for a tow."

"Or maybe they're waitin' for us." Parr gunned the engine and turned sharply into the driveway. "Damn Colombians. I'll teach 'em to spy on me. I shoulda listened to Blood. We don't need them after tonight. We'll take what we need and get rid of 'em for good."

Parr jerked Christy out of the back seat and led her to her room. He took off the cuffs and locked the door. She sank gratefully on the vile mattress. Her mind felt as numb as her wrists. Slowly, she felt the tingle of circulation as blood flowed back into her hands. Her mind cleared. The last few hours sank in.

Death. This day was surrounded by death, from the decay of Johnny Blue to the muffled outburst of Joey's handgun. Nothing in life had prepared her for today, or for the moment when death took the upper hand and came as close and as real as the point of a needle.

Less than an hour ago, she'd given up, surrendered to death while her spirit held fast to the last moments of life. There was nothing more she could do to save herself. The fight was over. It felt good, like exhaling after holding her breath five days too long.

But the protective mantle of shock was gone now, the numbness ebbed. Crouched on the mattress, Christy felt the events of the morning coming into harsh focus. She was back in the familiar room, still Parr's prisoner, but everything else had changed. She was a witness—and an outsider. Parr wouldn't release her now. Tomorrow's scenarios were whittled down to two possibilities: either Parr would kill the Colombians for the chemicals, or the Colombians would wipe out Parr's outfit for reneging on the deal. Either way, she would be in the crossfire.

From her despair, Christy felt the stirrings of an

emotion she couldn't easily identify. It wasn't fear. She was beyond the tentacles of fear at this point. It was pure and basic survival, the same instinct that made the coyote sacrifice its leg to escape a trap.

She sat upright on the bed and looked at her surroundings with new resolve. In the bathroom, she touched every inch of the space, pulling at pipes, testing the fixtures. A metal towel rack was loosely bolted to the wall. She forced it downward with her entire weight and rocked it until it fell free from the wall. Lightweight, but it would serve its purpose.

Leaving the bathroom, Christy eyed the bedroom closet with fresh interest. Up to now she had ignored the closet because the sliding door was off the top runner and jammed. She peered into the slight opening, but couldn't see anything. She tugged at the door and winced at its rusty squeal of resistance.

In the bathroom was Emilina's lilac scented soap. Christy took it and slowly, painstakingly, rubbed it over the rusted metal. Again, she tried to fit the closet back on the rollers. This time the metal was silent.

She worked the soap back and forth along the top runner, blocking out all thoughts except the task at hand. The lilac smell made her gag and soap flakes fell into her hair. She listened for footsteps down the hall, a key in the lock, but no one came to check on her. After easing the door back on the runners, Christy worked the soap along the bottom tracks, a fraction of an inch at a time, until the door opened wide enough to enter.

She put her head through the narrow opening for a look. The closet smelled of mold and mice droppings. There were no skeletons, much to her relief. In the corner sat a stack of comic books, partially shredded. An old shirt hung on a wire hanger. Christy pushed it to the far end of the rack. On the upper shelf were several shoe boxes which Christy checked, hoping to find a knife or gun. One contained a few photographs, sheets of paper scribbled with names and numbers, and a joint. The rest of the boxes were empty, their corners chewed by industrious mice.

She searched the ceiling and walls of the closet for access to an attic or crawlspace, but without a flashlight it was hard to determine if one existed. Grabbing the towel bar, Christy slid through the opening and eased her body to the far end of the closet. The dark, close space felt comforting. It was a cave, a niche created out of a need she responded to for a sense of safety. And control.

The first rays of daylight were filtering through the green curtains when she finished. Exhausted, Christy crawled out of the closet and sank down against the wall next to the door. Sleep came. The towel bar remained clutched in her fist.

CHAPTER 36

Parr was standing at the edge of the ditch. Christy held the rifle up and took aim. The shots sounded like caps from a toy gun. Her nose twitched at the acrid odor of gunpowder. Lloyd fell in slow motion and disappeared beneath the raging waters of the canal.

A second shot sounded and Christy woke from the short nap with a start. Every muscle in her body tensed, every nerve pricked like a thousand tiny needles. The rifle in her hands turned back into the towel bar. The dream was gone. The gunfire was real. The Colombians had arrived.

Christy dove into the closet and scrambled to the farthest corner. She snatched the wire clothes hanger from the pole overhead and let the shirt fall to the floor. She closed the door with her open palm, pleased as it slid smoothly on the track, satisfied with her handiwork. She jammed the wire hanger into the empty track and waited.

Through the door she heard muffled pounding. The alarm wailed into action. The darkness magnified and distorted the sound. Her own ragged breathing bounced off the closet walls.

The sound of wood splintering and a barrage of voices filled the hallway. Words filtered through the walls and lost coherence. Was it Spanish? She couldn't be sure. Fear made her ears buzz like a hive of bees lodged in her skull. She gripped the bar even tighter.

A thunderous crash jarred the walls and made the closet doors rattle on the track. The blackness of her hideaway became darker. Christy forced her eyes open and tensed, ready to strike.

For a few seconds, the only sound on the other side of the closet was the scuffling of footsteps. A light sliced through her cave and the sliding door jammed momentarily on the clothes hanger. Christy stood up, planted her feet, and held the bar above her head. The intruder pushed harder and the hanger gave under pressure. It sprang out of the runner and the door raced to the end of the track. Light streamed through the gap.

When she saw the head peer in, she swung down hard. The bar reverberated with contact. The man grabbed the closet door for support. Christy drew her weapon up for a second strike and stepped into the light.

The Dragon had a dazed look on his face and clutched his head. Christy ignored the sight of blood seeping through his fingers and concentrated on the weapon in his hand. She brought the bar down hard on his wrist and he dropped the gun. Then she swung the bar up and caught his lower jaw.

"Christy," he mumbled as he went down, "I came to save you."

On his entry vest were the letters "DEA."

The room suddenly filled with people—her people.

"Request Code Three ambulance, officer down. I'll be checking injuries," a hooded officer barked into his handset.

"Ten-four," responded the dispatcher.

Taking quick inventory of the fallen DEA agent, he keyed his handset. "Blunt instrument injury to head, face and arm. Subject semi-conscious and breathing. Go Code Four on regular traffic."

"Copy, Adam Twenty. I have paramedics in the area. Approximate ETA: eight minutes."

"Ten-Four."

Men in raid gear stared at her, a mixture of curiosity and concern painted their faces. Their chests heaved under bullet-proof vests as they struggled to come down from the adrenaline high. The musky odor of sweat enveloped the close space. She saw Sergeant Traynor push through the cluster until he was at her side. She felt his arm draw protectively around her as he gently pried the towel bar from her fingers.

A few faces from the substation came into focus. She spotted Wolfe standing by the window and locked onto his green eyes. There was guilt in those eyes, but she offered no absolution when she returned his gaze.

"You really went after Murietta," one of the men said to break the awkward tension. "Glad you're on our side."

"Better recruit her for SWAT, Sarge."

The sergeant took off his hood and she recognized Perrelli from the narcotics unit. "How did the Black Hearts survive a week around you?" he asked with a chuckle.

But Christy barely heard him. Her eyes focused on the man prone on the floor. A handkerchief stanched the blood from the gash on his head. His jaw was already discolored, and someone had packed ice on his wrist.

"I thought he was a Colombian drug dealer," she apologized to no one in particular. "I thought he was going to kill me."

"Agent Rod Murietta can be very convincing. He's one of the best—"

A siren cut Perrelli off. Paramedics rushed into the room.

Traynor led Christy outside. The pit bulls were sprawled in the driveway, shot cleanly through the head. Trimmer, Neeley, and Parr lay on the ground nearby, handcuffed, their faces in the dirt. Two deputies stood guard over each prisoner. Others scurried about in black mesh tops with "Central County Sheriff's Department" or "DEA" emblazoned on the back in day-glow yellow letters. Despite the unrelenting heat, narcs kept their faces hidden under black hoods. They looked like ninjas as they brought an arsenal of weapons out of the compound and spread the cache on the dirt driveway.

As the uniformed men in the yard became aware of her presence, they fell silent. Only their eyes and mouth were visible through their hoods. She shrank back, embarrassed to be seen looking so dirty. Traynor gave her a squeeze and kept his arm firmly around her shoulders. DEA Field Supervisor Monroe approached and motioned to follow him to the command center behind the bust van.

"We're glad to see you're safe and made it through this ordeal—" he began.

She cut him off. "Why did it take so long to rescue me?"

Monroe cleared his throat and glanced over at Traynor. The sergeant's cold stare let him know he wouldn't get any help fielding her question.

Monroe launched into official rhetoric. "We were involved in an ongoing investigation targeting Lloyd Parr's drug activities. When the hostage situation arose, we couldn't put our main objective in jeopardy." Monroe again cleared his throat and forced a tight smile. "Working for the sheriff's department, I'm sure you understand the priorities."

"I guess I wasn't one of your 'priorities,'" Christy said wearily.

Monroe appeared irritated by her lack of gratitude. "As I said, there were other considerations, other objectives in the operation. Your abduction was an unforseen and unfortunate event. But I would like to point out that you and Detective Wolfe are partially responsible for what occurred. Besides," he added, "we had constant surveillance on the area the entire time. We would have intervened if your life had really been in danger."

That did it. Christy strained against Traynor's hold. She wanted to wipe the smug look off Monroe's face with her fist. "They took me out on a back road yesterday and almost killed me with a drug overdose. Where were your men?"

For a split second, doubt crossed Monroe's face. It wasn't much, but Christy knew it was all she would get. Turning away, she looked out over the small army milling around the compound: DEA, BNE, ATF, sheriff's deputies, narcotics officers, local policemen. Parr and his gang had cost the government plenty in time and money. She felt overwhelmed by her own insignificance. To Monroe and his superiors, she'd been a wrench thrown into the works of a much bigger plan.

The paramedics carried Luis Mondragon, AKA Rod Murietta, out on a stretcher. Even with his arm in a pressure bandage and his forehead wrapped in gauze, he was handsome. Christy felt something stir inside at the sight of him, and this time she gave herself permission to enjoy it. Knowing the Dragon was DEA instead of a drug lord only stoked the fire. She was sorry she'd beaten him so badly, but at the same time proud she'd defended herself so well. He gave her a wink and a thumbs up as they carried him away. She beamed at his accolade and watched as the ambulance left the scene.

Three sheriff's patrol cars drove up to the house. Parr and his men were pulled to their feet and each led to a separate car. Trimmer tried to shake off the hands that firmly held him, spewing insults and obscenities with every step. Joey went quietly. Neeley's swagger dissolved when he stumbled and hit his head entering the car door. Pausing for a moment, Parr glanced back at her, at the sergeant's arm encircling her shoulders, and a rueful smile played on his lips. She knew he was trying to put the puzzle together.

She watched as the units drove out of the compound and headed for the county jail in Kearny. Agents and detectives shed their forty-pound vests and pulled off their hoods with relief. Sweat poured from their faces.

"I know you want to get home. Lennie's anxious to see you," Traynor said as he finally released her from his grasp. "Just a few more ends to tie up here and I'll take you home."

Christy nodded wearily and sank down on a tree

stump to wait. She watched as men came out of the house carrying notebooks of pay/owe lists from dealers and clients, several bongs, a dope scale, and Parr's enamel stash box.

Activity swirled around her, but Christy felt detached, almost invisible. She realized she should feel elated, but all she felt was hunger, fatigue, and very, very dirty. A migraine formed behind her left eye. Sitting in the broiling mid-morning sun brought it on faster. Her aching muscles cried out for a cool bubble bath and a soft bed, not necessarily in that order. Those were her priorities, and she wouldn't really feel free until they were met.

Perrelli, Traynor, and Monroe stood a short distance away. Perrelli had a cell phone to his ear.

"Team two is at the Perez house, they have Emilina in custody without incident," Perrelli announced. He held his handset up to his ear. "Team three, at the Youngblood trailer, wife in custody. No sign of Youngblood."

"Where the hell did Youngblood disappear to?" Monroe asked the sergeants in exasperation.

"He's dead."

The three men turned toward her and, once again, she was the focus of their attention. Traynor walked over and crouched down in front of her.

"How do you know, Christy?"

"I was there." She felt her throat tighten, as if to choke back the memory. "They pushed his body into a dry canal. They left him there with Johnny Blue." Tears welled unexpectedly. A single drop trickled down her dirty cheek.

Mention of the snitch's name startled Wolfe. "You'll have to take us back to the canal," he said. "Can you do that, Christy?"

She looked at him reproachfully. She felt pushed beyond endurance. "I want to go home."

Traynor roughly pushed Wolfe out the way. "I know. And we want to take you home. But first, you need to help us find those bodies."

If Perrelli or Monroe had made the request, she would have refused. Traynor was the only one who could ask her to relive the nightmare. She couldn't turn down her sergeant. She rose on unsteady legs and took a deep breath. "We don't have much time. Parr said the water gates are scheduled to be opened. If that happens, the bodies will be washed downstream."

CHAPTER 37

Perrelli talked maniacally into his handset. "Get the homicide lieutenant on land-line to my cell phone and tell him I have two possible bodies in the south county area. Contact the Water District and tell them to close the reservoir gates. Emergency status. Say the orders came from Sheriff Nolan. And I want the dive team on standby."

Finished with dispatch for the time being, Perrelli pulled a map of Central County out of his briefcase and spread it on the hood of his car. He motioned Christy over. "Show us where you saw the bodies."

She stared blankly at the sprawl of intersecting lines covering the paper and shook her head. "I can't find it on a map. I just know where it is. At least, I think I know."

Traynor intervened. "Do you mean, you think you can find the irrigation ditch from memory?"

"I remember landmarks."

Perrelli covered his eyes. "This isn't going to work. We're going to lose the evidence."

"It'll work," Traynor said as he folded up the map.

Christy heard the forced optimism in his voice, grateful for his support.

Perrelli picked up his handset and keyed dispatch again. "Find out if Highway Patrol has a 'copter up. If not, notify the air squadron that we need a bird in the sky in twenty minutes."

"Copy," came the tired reply.

Perrelli commandeered two undercover vehicles and a patrol unit. Traynor hoisted his bulk into the backseat of Perrelli's T-Bird. Wolfe pulled up beside them in the Crankmobile.

"Where the hell do you think you're going, Detective?" Perrelli asked.

"Blue was my snitch, Sarge. I'm the only one who can identify the body."

The narcotics sergeant gave Wolfe an icy look. "All right. But let me lay it out for you, Detective. After we wrap this case, I'm giving you a choice. You can go back to patrol, or face an Internal Affairs investigation. Either way, you're out of the unit."

Perrelli hit the gas pedal before Wolfe could reply. The spinning tires kicked up a cloud of dust in its wake. Christy saw Wolfe's dumb-struck expression recede in the haze. What did he expect—a commendation? Finally, he would pay for his manipulations. It was going to cost him his detective badge

She pushed away any feelings of remorse for her ex-boyfriend and concentrated on the task ahead. Could she pull this off? Images from yesterday's terrifying journey scrambled in her head, some clearer than others. Sensing her self-doubts, Traynor reached over the seat and gave her shoulder a reassuring pat.

Perrelli turned to Christy. He idled the T-Bird at the entrance to the compound as he waited for her directions.

"We went out the back way, through the rows of grapes. When we got to a main road, I remember passing a white church. It had a large steeple with four smaller steeples, one on each corner."

Both men furrowed their brows in concentration. "It's gotta be the Trinity Church. What side of the road was it on, Christy?" Traynor asked.

"The left."

"Here goes nothing," Perrelli muttered. He grabbed the mic of his car radio and spoke to the vehicles behind the T-Bird. "Heading south bound on McCall. Wait for further instructions."

All Christy remembered of the church was the portion she saw from her half-prone position in the pickup. When a steeple matching her description rose into view, relief flooded over her. Perrelli slowed down and all the cars in the entourage slowed down behind them. Quickly, she searched her mind for the next clue.

"We passed a graveyard up ahead on the right-hand side of the road."

"Guadalupe Cemetery." The sergeant pressed on the gas and called out over the radio, "Proceed to McCall and American."

The cars trailed to the location and lined up at the stop sign, ready for further instructions.

Perrelli drummed his fingers on the steering wheel. "Well?"

Christy looked around. Youngblood had made a turn, maybe to the left, but not this early in the ride. "Keep going straight." Her voice wavered.

Perrelli caught it. "How far?"

"I don't know. We turned, but I don't know exactly where."

The dispatcher's voice cut through the dead air in the car. "CHP helicopter is in the area, requests you make contact on channel fifteen."

Perrelli cruised through the stop sign and pulled off the road in front of the graveyard to let traffic pass. The other three cars pulled onto the shoulder behind him. A family paying their respects stared curiously at the procession.

"Adam Fifteen to CHP. We need assistance locating a homicide site in the south county area."

"Copy, Kearny Sheriff's. What are we looking for?"

Perrelli glanced skeptically at Christy. "Got any landmarks I can give the pilot?"

"There was an old barn by the canal."

Perrelli caught himself in mid-curse. "There are hundreds of old barns around here."

She closed her eyes and pictured the vineyards and the oak standing guard over the two corpses. Her mind tried to block the image, but she bit her lip and forced herself to go back to the moment when she waited for death. She reached out and found the last image etched in her mind.

Remember this.

"Tell them to look for a stand of seven palm trees, all in a line. One will be taller than the rest."

"What direction?"

She visualized the late-morning sun topping the tallest fronds. "East."

Perrelli looked at her for the first time with a hint of respect in his eyes. He keyed the mic. "Airborne, head east from McCall and try to spot a line of palms with one tall one in the group. We'll need a fix on that location."

"Ten-four. What are we on, a scavenger hunt?"

"Roger that. See what you can find for us."

Perrelli pulled off the gravel shoulder and floored the pedal with the insolence of a man immune to speeding tickets. The Thunderbird sped alongside a rock and cement canal. Water gushed through the gates and cascaded into the irrigation canal. The ditch was already up to a third of its capacity, and filling fast. All three passengers took uneasy notice as the churning water raced to get to the bodies first.

The cars approached a stop sign.

"Is this the turn?" Perrelli pressed. She nodded. One at a time, the cars pulled up to the four-way, waited for farm machinery and vans of pickers to pass, then turned onto Adams Avenue.

"Adam Fifteen, this is Delta Thirty." Homicide detective Jimmy Kerwin's voice crackled over the radio. "We'll be joining you. ETA ten minutes."

"Roger, Delta Thirty. Welcome to the party."

Orchards spun past, grapevines, ramshackle farmhouses, a hill of tires dumped by the railroad tracks. It looked identical to dozens of county roads. A mirage of water on the asphalt shimmered in the distance as the sun blazed on the road and heat rose into the air in waves. Christy felt pale and clammy. A familiar queasiness welled up inside her. She reached for the air conditioning vent and leaned into the cold rush of air. Something beyond car sickness took hold.

"Turn back."

Perrelli jerked his head toward her. "Is this the wrong road?"

"Please. Turn around. I've made a mistake. I can't

find it." Her breath came in quick, sharp gasps.

"This is CHP Air," interrupted the radio. "We spotted some palm trees, but they're in rows, not a line. One is definitely taller."

"What's your fix on the location?"

"Just north of Manning, possibly Lac Jac Avenue."

Perrelli set his jaw. "Hold your position. We're en route."

The convoy passed farm laborers, who gawked at the sudden influx of traffic on the quiet country road, preparing to run if an Immigration van appeared. The stutter of helicopter blades beat the air as it passed overhead. Christy clawed at the seatbelt as the car continued to race forward against her wishes.

"She's hyperventilating. Traynor, get her under control."

Christy felt Traynor's beefy hands on her shoulders as he pulled her back in the seat. His soothing voice instructed her to cup her hands over her mouth and take slow, deep breaths. She did as she was told. Her eyes came back into focus.

The T-Bird passed a large ranch house.

"Look." Perrelli pointed at the horizon.

Rising above the acres of vines, looking like a desert oasis, seven palms swayed in the hot breeze. Even from the distance, it was easy to see one of the spindly trees towered over the others. Christy shrank from the sight as memories flooded back. A helicopter circled the stand of palms.

"Okay CHP, we've got you in our sights. Fly west bound and spot us to a barn with a canal running by it."

The pilot turned the chopper gracefully and flew toward them. All the cars halted in the road and a small, confused traffic jam built up behind them. Homicide was at the tail end of the mess and radioed impatiently as to the hold up. Perrelli ignored them.

"I see the barn and canal," announced the pilot. "There are three entry points east of your location. Unable to tell which road will get you to the site."

"Copy, and thanks for the assist." Perrelli slowed to thirty miles per hour but managed to overshoot the first road, which was camouflaged by vines. Wolfe pulled into the narrow opening and disappeared. Perrelli made the second turn-off and the patrol unit passed them on its way to the third road.

Fine, thin branches of grapevine whipped at the sides of the T-Bird. The car lurched over the rutted road until it finally broke free of leafy tentacles and burst into a clearing.

The barn loomed up, weathered and foreboding. Christy sat, immobile, staring at the site. It looked like an empty movie set, but her mind supplied the actors: Trimmer, Neeley, Joey, Emilina, Parr, and Youngblood.

All units were ordered to meet at the barn.

"Christy." Traynor shook her lightly on the shoulder. "We have to get out."

She stirred, fearful that her legs would betray her. Finally, she unbuckled the seat belt and slid out of the car. Heat washed over her. She grabbed Traynor's arm for support.

"We got the remains of two over here," Detective Kerwin called out.

With morbid curiosity, deputies swarmed to the canal and peered over the side for a look at the Blue's skeleton and the day-old corpse of Youngblood. A few lost their breakfast behind the oak.

I-Bureau showed up.

"We already got a few feet of water, folks, so get your pictures but make it fast," Kerwin barked. "We've got to get these stiffs on dry land."

Christy watched as people she hardly knew in the sheriff's department went about their jobs. Cameras flashed, detectives wrote furiously in notebooks, different areas were measured. It was grisly business as usual.

How much different would they act if it was her body they were fishing out of the canal?

Eventually, the brass made an appearance, including Sheriff Nolan. He eyed Christy curiously, but didn't approach. The media was already en route, pushing to film the noon telecast and a teaser for the evening news.

She felt a rough hand on her shoulder.

Traynor guided her to a waiting patrol car. "You did a real good job, Christy. I think it's time we got you out of here before the media shows up."

She did not look back.

CHAPTER 38

Traynor hit the siren as he entered the circle drive of 1331 Raisin Ridge. Lennie was wheeled out of the house in a wheelchair, her right leg elevated. A strange man navigated the wheelchair down a makeshift ramp to the driveway. Mrs. Alcorn followed. Even Jonathan Maciel put in an appearance as part of the welcoming committee.

"Oh, Christy!" Lennie choked and couldn't get any more words out. She spread her arms and Christy walked into a hug of tourniquet proportions. A second later, Lennie pushed her away. "Whew! You need a hot shower and scrub down with Lysol! You're a week's worth of ripe!"

Leave it to Lennie to verbalize the obvious. No wonder the deputies gave her wide berth. Christy had become accustomed to the feel of filthy clothes sticking to her body, limp and knotted hair, and the acrid odor of perspiration clinging to her like cheap cologne.

She backed away and pointed to the cast on Lennie's leg. "What happened to you?" she said, changing the subject.

"I tried to save you and got into a little car accident. This—" Lennie jerked her thumb in the direction of the tall man behind her holding on to the handles of the chair, "—is Teddy. Dr. Brant. He's my angel of mercy and promised to stay by my bedside until my leg fracture heals."

"Which should be in about an hour." Teddy Brant came around the chair and hunkered down to look Lennie in the eye. "There's nothing wrong with your leg. The DEA made me put you in a cast to keep you from interfering with their investigation. Now that your roommate's rescued, I can take the cast off anytime."

Christy watched Lennie struggle to keep from spewing out a few choice cuss words. But she also noticed how quickly Lennie forgave the doctor for his role in the charade.

"Before I get back on my feet, I have something important to tell you." Lennie looked over Christy's shoulder at Sergeant Traynor. He attempted to keep a straight face as he gave her a little nod.

Lennie looked deeply into Christy's weary eyes. "Do you remember the horoscope you did for me, the part where you said I would inherit some money?"

"Oh, Lennie, I'm too tired for this right now. I don't care if I ever see another horoscope again."

"If you think a lot has happened to you in five days, wait until you hear what happened to me. My whole life changed while you were stuck in that rat hole. I'm glad you're home to enjoy it with me because it sure would be lousy without you." Lennie leaned out in the chair and grabbed Christy's wrist. "I'm rich, girl. And not just a little rich, either. I'm filthy, stinkin' rich." She paused to gauge Christy's reaction. "What you saw in the horoscope was true. My aunt Leonida died, and because I'm her namesake, she made me her heir."

Christy interrupted. "Your real name is Leonida?"

"I legally changed it, and don't you tell a soul! Anyway, Aunt Leonida worked for years for a struggling coffee importer up in Seattle. There were times he was too broke to pay her, so he gave her stock instead. Who knew that coffee would suddenly take off and become hot stuff in the nineties?"

Even through overpowering fatigue, the words registered. "You don't mean…"

"You're lookin' at the major stockholder of Mt. Rainer Coffee." Lennie beamed up at her. "I'm rich beyond anything you coulda predicted. 'Course, I haven't got my hands on the cash yet, but I got a slew of lawyers ready to do anything to keep me happy."

The news overwhelmed Christy. So much had happened in so little time. She felt the weight of the whole week pressing down on her. "I'm thrilled for you, Lennie. But this is too much all at once. I've had a rough week. All I want to do now is get out of these filthy clothes and lay down in my own bed."

But Lennie wasn't finished. "I've been learning money talks real loud." She motioned to Teddy and he propelled the wheelchair toward the parking stalls in the rear of the house. She still had her hand clamped on Christy's wrist, pulling her along. Traynor, Mrs. Alcorn, and Mr. Maciel followed like a parade. "I told the lawyers I wanted to reward my astrologer, and they advanced me some cash, even though the legal stuff isn't wrapped up yet."

The group turned the corner and there, in Christy's stall where the Fiat usually sat leaking oil, stood a midnight blue Saturn. Christy stared, but didn't comprehend.

"I asked myself, 'What kind of car would an astrologer drive?' and this it was either this, a Mercury, or a Ford Taurus." Lennie dangled a set of car keys in front or Christy's face. "I also ordered fancy personalized plates to read 'STARGZR.' They're coming in a couple of weeks."

Dazed, Christy accepted the keys. Traynor tugged the ribbon free from the door. New car smell enveloped her as she reached in and stroked the dove-gray upholstery. She wanted to jump into the driver's seat, but seven days of dirt on her body held her back.

Christy saw Lennie's Volvo still parked in the stall. "You bought me a car and didn't buy one for yourself?"

"Don't worry about me. Aunt Leonida's vintage Jaguar is being shipped from Seattle as soon as the estate's settled." Lennie grinned. "I'm real sorry I didn't know my aunt, but we must've been a lot alike. I've always had a hankering to drive a Jag."

"Christy, I have a surprise for you too." Mrs. Alcorn held out a wicker picnic basket with a green bow on the handle. The lid bobbed up and a pink nose peeked out. Two gray eyes came into view as the lid rose higher.

"I found your kitty. I told you he would be back. All it took was a little cream to coax him out of the bushes."

"Oh, Mrs. Alcrn, we don't own—" Lennie began, but it was too late.

The kitten was in Christy's arms and purring as smoothly as the new car engine.

"Thanks for finding him, Mrs. Alcorn. And thanks for passing the message on to Lennie."

"Oh, I didn't mind at all. By the way, does the kitty have a name? If he gets lost again, he might come if I call his name."

Christy thought for a minute. The cat had been the only clue she could think of to alert Lennie she'd been kidnaped.

"Shamus. That's his name. Isn't it, boy?" she said to the kitten. "But don't worry, Mrs. Alcorn. I don't think any of us will get lost again."

ოჯოჯ

Before heading back to the substation, Traynor told Christy she was needed back at Headquarters for debriefing at 1800 hours. The news didn't thrill her, but she knew the drill: debrief while the memories were fresh. She thanked the sergeant for his help, thanked the neighbors for their concern, thanked Lennie for the car, and thanked God she was home.

The claw-footed bathtub looked more inviting than the bed. Filling it with hot water, Christy squeezed out an extra dollop of strawberry scented bubble bath. The kitten watched intently, mesmerized by the foam. She shampooed under the spigot then eased back against the bath pillow and felt all the dirt and tension of the past week float free from her body. When images of the locked room and Youngblood's cold eyes intruded, she sank lower in the tub until her hair fanned out like seaweed and bubbles tickled her nose. It would be awhile before all the demons were gone. She'd face them one at a time.

I never left you.

Her sister's voice sounded clear in her head.

"I know, Celeste. I felt your prayers."

I'm glad you're safe. I'm glad you're home.

Christy reached out and gave Shamus a wet pat. "Me too."

ભૂલ

She was drying off when the telephone rang. She wrapped the towel around her body and picked up the phone in the kitchen. Her mother's voice cackled through the receiver.

"I just wanted to remind you that your sister's Feast Day is coming up. You need to be sure and send her a card. Try not to be late again this year," Mrs. Bristol chided.

Even being badgered by her mother felt good.

"Right Mom. I'll get to a card shop this week."

"They're a little hard to find, so save yourself some time and call the shops first."

Christy could feel herself fading out of the conversation. "I promise to look."

"Your grandmother called last week asking about you. She had a dream of you fighting a dragon with a knitting needle. Isn't that silly? You don't even knit!"

So Grandma Good had tapped in too. Christy should've expected it. The psychic ties were blood-strong. "I'll drop Grandma a letter and let her know I'm doing fine."

Shamus picked that moment to let out a hungry and insistent meow.

"Is that a cat?" Her mother sounded incredulous. "When did you get a cat? You shouldn't have an animal in an apartment. You'll have to get the thing declawed and the house will smell of litterbox—"

"Mom, I've never had a pet before." Christy was met with silence on the other end of line. "His name is Shamus," she continued, "and I'm keeping him. I have to go now."

Christy hung up the phone and headed to the comfort of her bed. The kitten curled up in the curve of her body. She put her hand under his tummy and cuddled him like a plush toy. In seconds, she fell into the first deep sleep she'd had in a week.

Pleasures, gifts, romance, and flirtations are possible under the influence of Venus.

CHAPTER 39

All too soon it was five p.m. Christy knew she could function on four hours of sleep, but it took all her will power to leave the comfort of her bed. Mrs. Alcorn knocked on her door with a ham sandwich and potatoes chips, and Mr. Maciel brought a pitcher of fresh-squeezed lemonade.

Lennie, she was told, had left with Dr. Teddy to get rid of the cast on her leg.

Christy brushed out her hair and styled it with the blow dryer. She applied a little concealer to disguise the abuses of the past week.

She slid her closet door open and buried her face in the racks of clean, fresh-smelling clothes. The jeans and top she'd worn at Parr's house were on their way to the garbage. Or maybe she would burn them.

Lennie and Teddy drove up just as Christy climbed

into the driver's seat of the Saturn. It felt like she was entering the cockpit of a jet.

"Wait! I want to be your first passenger." Lennie climbed into the car and gave the doctor an air kiss goodbye.

Christy concentrated on driving through rush hour traffic in downtown Kearny. As she pulled into the underground garage, several deputies gassing up their patrol cars gave a nod of recognition. It didn't take long for word to get around at the sheriff's department.

Traynor and Perrelli, the strain of the day evident on their faces, were on overtime waiting in the watch commander's office. They pointed to the room where the debriefing would take place then disappeared.

"I'll just visit with the girls in Records and rustle up a couple of Dr Peppers for us," Lennie said as she patted Christy on the arm.

Christy knocked lightly and heard a voice reply, "Come in." She opened the door slowly, not sure whether to expect a panel of stern-faced men ready to grill her, or a naked light bulb with a chair under it like the movies.

He sat on one side of a long table, papers neatly stacked in front of him, a gold pen resting exactly parallel to the papers. A carafe of water and two plastic cups were in the middle of the table, within easy reach for both. He stood up as she walked in and his eyes appraised her. The fresh bandage on one side of his forehead gave him a rakish air.

"I don't think we got a chance to be properly introduced," he said, holding out his hand. "I'm Rod Murietta."

"I'm sorry about your head," Christy murmured.

He grinned. "Injured in the line of duty."

For the first half hour, Agent Murietta was professional and struggled to maintain a certain detachment as he prodded Christy into remembering details of the Parr compound. The conversation was being taped, but Agent Murietta also took detailed notes. Sometimes his pen would hesitate as she recalled how Youngblood had roughed her up for talking to his son, or how they discussed killing her right in front of her. Christy fought to keep her composure and tried to be as professional as the man across from her.

"What will happen to Joey Youngblood?" she ventured to ask as Murietta's questions wound down.

"He has a fairly clean record. But murdering his father is going to look pretty bad in court."

"Even if he did it to save my life?"

Murietta searched her eyes. "I could go to the judge and tell him the circumstances. Maybe with a written statement from you, he'll take it under consideration."

It was the least she could do for the boy. "And what about Emilina?"

"Well, we have kidnaping charges against her." He looked at her curiously. "She wanted you dead, you know."

"She brought me things." Christy brushed sudden tears from her eyes at the thought of Emilina's small acts of kindness. "Parr and his men used her. I think she was just as much a victim as I was."

Murietta handed her a tissue from a box next to his briefcase on the floor. "Maybe we could plea bargain down to charges of conspiracy. Anything else?"

Something had been bothering Christy, but it embarrassed her to ask. "I looked up info on the Black Hearts before I did the horoscope. I know it was wrong to use the data base for my own purposes. But a name stuck in my head, so when they pushed me to tell them who put me up to casting Parr's horoscope, I told them it was Trace Malin. Then he showed up and went along with my story. That's the only reason I'm still alive."

Murietta smiled. "Trace thinks fast on his feet. He filled us in on your situation. We had him released from prison to work as a confidential, paid informant on the case. Your abduction upped our time-line and put our plan in high gear."

The interview was over. Along with a sense of relief was an odd sadness. She watched as he cleaned off the table and put the paperwork in his briefcase. The click of the lock signaled that it was over. He'd saved her life, but it was time to move on.

Christy turned and let herself out of the room.

೮ಎ೮ಎ

The Saturn streaked down Highway 41. The silhouette of grapevines contrasted the moonlit night. Christy drove more confidently than she ever had in the Fiat. The Saturn felt sleek and powerful, and she experienced a sense of abandon that wasn't there five days ago.

"Can I turn on the radio?" Lennie reached for the knob.

"No," answered Christy. "I want to listen to the car."

Lennie cocked her head. "I don't hear anything."

"Exactly."

They rode in silence, Christy content to feel the Saturn respond to the subtlest turn of the wheel, the lightest touch on the gas pedal. Lennie shifted uncomfortably.

"Traynor says not to bother you with a lot of questions. He says you'll talk about it when you're ready."

Christy nodded. "He thinks I ought to visit the department shrink."

"I just want you to know I did everything I could think of to get you back. Everybody did." Lennie looked out the side window at the grapevines. "I also want you to know I'm going to quit working as soon as I get the money. I'm not good at the job. Anyway, it seems silly to be a rich working girl."

They drove home in silence. As they entered their apartment, the telephone was ringing.

"For you," Lennie said, handing her the phone.

His voice sounded too intimate in the close confines

of the receiver. "Christy, you bolted from the room be-fore I was finished. There's just one more thing I need to ask you." Rod Murietta's voice had the low purr of the Dragon again.

"Yes?"

"My horoscope—did you ever get a chance to do it?"

Christy cradled the phone on her shoulder and smiled. He wasn't asking about the Black Hearts or the lab operation. He wanted to know what everybody want-ed to know when they found out she was an astrologer.

"Yes, I did."

"Was there anything in my horoscope you want to tell me about?"

She could feel a blush moving up her neck and turn-ing to fire on her cheeks.

"This is hard over the phone," he said, misinterpret-ing her silence. "Maybe we can discuss it over dinner. Are you doing anything Saturday night?"

Christy hadn't seen this in his horoscope. She smiled. Maybe she'd better re-check her own chart. She had a hunch Saturday nights, and her future, would never be boring again.

About the Author

Sunny Frazier trained as a journalist and wrote for a city newspaper, military, and law enforcement publications. After working 17 years with the Fresno Sheriff's Department, 11 spent as a Girl Friday with an undercover narcotics team, it dawned on her that mystery writing was her real calling. Both *Fools Rush In* and *Where Angels Fear* are based on actual cases with a bit of astrology, a habit Frazier has developed over the past 43 years.

www.ingramcontent.com/pod-product-compliance
Lightning Source LLC
Chambersburg PA
CBHW060532180626
46817CB00002B/539